Single Mums

Gawd Bless 'Em

Mo Lily

Single Mums – Gawd Bless 'em

5op
42

For Beryl

Single Mums – Gawd Bless 'em

'What about the women?' you asked.
Well here it is.
You know who you are.

If ego can ego mos
If I can I will

Single Mums – Gawd Bless 'em

Characters

Jenny - One Boy

Sarah - Two Girls

Sadie - One Girl One Boy

Ruth - One Girl

Jackie - One Boy and a Mum

Single Mums – Gawd Bless 'em

Chapter One

I quickly pulled my knickers back on, peeing in the bushes, in the dark, was not pleasant.

'Hurry up.' Sarah called out to me as she pressed on her car hooter. That's it draw attention to ourselves. My four-inch heels kept sinking into the mud and long grass. I scrambled back into her minuscule wreck of a car, full to capacity with similar girls, er, women as myself.

I am thirty-two, a single mum. As we all are, single mums, not all thirty-two, Jackie is into her forties though she would never admit to it. I climbed into the back seat, only two doors on this thing, gosh, I wish I had driven.

They made room for me but moaned as the car chugged off with a great effort.

'She drank too much.'

'It's not how much, it's those long drinks she has, why can't she have shorts like us?'

'Do you mind not talking about me as if I am not here?' I uncomfortably told them.

Southern Comfort and lemonade was my drink choice, they did always drown it in lemonade, and I had only had three drinks tonight, but that is a pint and a half of lemonade. They last me all evening whereas if I had just Comfort on its own, two sips and it would gone, and I would be looking round for another.

'I feel sick' said Sadie.

'For Christ's sake we are not stopping again.'

'Supposing I am sick?'

'Not in here you're not,' said the driver 'I'll stop.'

'I think I'll be alright.' Sadie meekly said.

We were on our way to a party.

'You sure you know the way?' Sarah asked Ruth as she was peering out the windscreen, there were no streetlights, 'I didn't know it was this far.'

'Yes, keep going.'

In the pub, Ruth had met an ex-boyfriend

who invited us back to his place for this party.

Taking the short ride to our local drinking area in this heap of a car was not too bad but coming all this way into the country, no streetlights, just little lanes, narrow I mean, not short, they go on forever. Posh expensive looking houses everywhere, this is madness.

I tried to wipe my heels on Sarah's already filthy carpet.

'Not far, slow down a bit.' Impossible for Sarah, neither she, nor her car could manage slowly.

'Here, here, left, do a left,' shouted Ruth. Sarah skidded the car around the corner, doing the left turn as requested.

'Slowly!' We all shouted at her.

'Okay. It is very dark I can't see any numbers what side of the road is this house?'

'There look.' As we turned a bend, we could see a house looking like Blackpool Tower, every light on in the place. Sarah drove the car, up the curb and onto the front lawn, the drive was full. I felt I needed to pee again. I hoped I was not getting that bladder infection back again.

Tumbling out of the death trap, we pulled down our skirts and tucked up hair patting it into place. Sticking our chests out, we entered the affray.

What a load of toffs, not my cup of tea at all, I like my crowd rough, not common rough, hoods or crooks, just uneducated I suppose but not short of a few bob. It was a nice enough house if it wasn't for the magnolia paint everywhere and carpets to match. I tried to give my muddy heels another wipe before putting a foot on it.

'Whose house is this?' I asked.

'Jeff's parents.'

'He still lives at home with mummy?'

'No he has his own flat in town.'

'Oh he would.' Jeff was short and almost fat, heading that way, his hair he had cut very short as he was losing it. Not the sort you would look at twice unless you could see the money beyond his looks.

Then there was his personality, such a nice chap, pleasant to talk too, showed interest in what you were saying however trivial. He listened with an intent that all else disappeared into the background and he made you feel alone with him. He was nowhere to be seen in this vast house.

There were many people, strangers to me, all standing, talking about nothing. A girl was sleeping on the sofa, taking up much room.

A dog, a large golden retriever wandered amongst the crowd, wagging his tail nonstop, pleased to see everyone but really looking to snatch a morsel of food.

'You shouldn't let the dog in here Jeff' a women called from somewhere 'mother will go mad.' Go mad at the dog what about all these people on her carpet.

'No red wine.' I heard the same voice tell a person searching amongst the bottles of booze.

'Have you run out?'

'No dear, wandering around carrying a glass of red wine, the carpet you know.'

I had to find the loo, all these drinks around me made it worse I needed to go now. Off the hall a little queue had formed, that must be it. Going to the front, I asked could I go next as I was desperate.

'We all are darling take your turn.' A posh voice, but a common shit, told me dismissing my request. Before I peed on mummy's carpet I went upstairs, this sort of house had an en suite bathroom off every bedroom.

The first door I opened, there in front of me lying on the end of the bed was a girl without a stitch on, her arms spread wide, she stared with a nonchalant look, at a bloke. He, fully dressed, was standing on the floor at the end of the bed, holding her legs high over his shoulders, they were at it, well he was.

'Sorry.' I blurted and left them to it, I don't think they noticed me anyway, he certainly didn't pause in his rhythm. The next room was empty and had a smart loo. Relieving myself was a relief, huh. I made a mental note no more lemonade, stupid stuff anyway, far too gassy.

I made my way back to the busy room, found Sarah and stood beside her. She was talking and laughing with strangers. During a gap in her conversation, only a slight pause.

'Have you seen Jeff?' I asked her.

'Jeff who?' Came the reply, then she continued her boring conversation. I didn't want to be here, I was tired. It sounded a good idea at the time, the whole evening sounded a good idea, it always does, get out have a break.

Spending ages getting ready, rushing as I have a ten-year-old son to care for in between sorting myself out. My sister was sleeping over with her son, almost the same age as my Tommy, they would have a good time probably better than I was. Then I would have to repay Sis and do the same for her, it just goes on and on.

I stood beside Sarah in silence, not listening, but laughing when she did. I picked fault, what a toff, what a tart, what a pig, when was someone nice going to appear.

'Do you want to go?' asked Sarah.

'I'm all right' I lied. I had best move around a bit, go and find the kitchen see if there is any grub going. Strange that I should think the kitchen would be empty, it was another room crammed with false laughter. No food, never had been or had it all long gone.

'Jeff' called the voice. Oh, there he is, he really is very short, it must be all his money in his pockets weighting him down. Shame to be rich and ugly, and then if he were good looking he would be objectionable.

I went back to my place next to Sarah who gave me a "go away" look as she was talking to a good looker. I eyed him with suspicion and went away.

Where were the other girls? Jackie had found 'her' on the sofa, shoved her legs up under her chin and made room for her own arse on the edge looking like I felt, bored.

'All right love?' She asked as I approached, 'she is an air stewardess, she's had no sleep for a couple of nights, just got back from Cairo.' She pointed to the sleeping body. I gave the girl a good look, very pretty, great legs tucked up in such a way you could see her white lace draws a little. How could she sleep there, why didn't she find a comfortable bed upstairs.

'She belongs to him.' Jackie pointed to a chap who kept glancing over at the sleeping beauty. Some oaf, as he passed, smacked her bum, not so lightly".

'Wake up darling you are missing all the fun.' He told her.

'Leave her Hugh' called her watchful chaperone. I looked around for the fun she was missing, still holding my glass of white wine, white because of mummy's carpet, untouched because of my bladder. It must be an infection my tummy felt sore.

'Ready for the off?' Asked Sarah as her good looker had dismissed her. I said, "Okay" though I wanted to say, "Yes please".

'Round em up ducks.'

'Me?' I had not seen Ruth or Sadie, our other two squashed in the car companions, since we arrived. I pushed amongst the drinkers looking for them.   Ruth was talking to her ex, Jeff. Sadie was snogging a "thing" in an armchair, had she taken a good look at him?

'We are going Sadie.' I shouted in her ear, as she took no notice of me tapping her shoulder. Surfacing a little, she sees me.

'Okay love, bye.'

'What! Are you staying here?'

'May as well.'

'You sure?'

'Yes, very sure.' She went back to the "thing" and carried on with what they were doing before I interrupted them.

'We are going you do understand?'

'Mm' came the reply.

Sarah looked worried when I told her, and stared in her direction.

'She is a grown woman it is up to her, come on.' As I put my full-untouched glass down a hand came on my arm.

'May I give you my card?' The face that went with the hand said to me. Do what you like mate, I thought and took it as I looked into the most beautiful eyes with long lashes that any girl would die for, imagine how long you could make them with mascara, totally wasted on this bloke, or on any bloke.

'If you want.' I so intelligently said to the eyes, taking a swift glance up and down the body, not bad, two legs, and two arms.

'Goodnight.' I told him, there manners, he smiled at me. I stuffed his card into my skirt pocket along with my keys, my hanky, money and mobile phone, making it bulge out in a peculiar way. Should have brought my shoulder bag.

We left. There was a little more room in the back of the car now, thank goodness and Jackie was soon asleep leaning on me.

'I'm sorry I have gone wrong haven't I?' said Ruth, 'it should have been a right not a left as we turned in we did a left wasn't it going there, not right?' she was waving and bending her hands, 'a left I said left didn't I?'

'Shut up you stupid bitch.' Sarah was getting cross 'I just hope I have enough petrol to get us home.'

'Don't keep going then Sare, turn round and go back, start again.' I told her.

'I can't turn round in this silly lane it's not wide enough I would end up in a ditch.' She found a farm entrance, reversed into it banging the gate with her car bumper as she did, we returned to where we started.

Why do people want to live in the country, give me towns and streetlights any day.

'Night love, I'll phone you tomorrow.' Sarah said as I climbed out of her car, her last drop off. I gave her a brief kiss on the cheek and crept indoors, taking my still muddy high heels off first. Was it worth it?

My sister was asleep in the spare bed. Tuck her son was in Tommy's room, my sister is Mrs Tucker, we had always called her son little Tuck, his dad being big Tuck.

A little line under the top line of the T for Tucker was what my sister felt more appropriate for her husband's name. She did not get on with him. He thought she did as he got on with her quite nicely but her "little line" as he was known did not come up to her expectation. Now little Tuck was a different kettle of fish she adored him. He was sleeping in the bottom bunk in Tommy's room.

After checking on all this I made a hot water bottle for my aching tummy, chucked my clothes off and left them where they fell, emptying my pockets on to the dressing table. Grabbed some pyjamas did yet another pee, did not clean my teeth or remove my makeup.

As I went off to sleep cuddling my soothing hot water bottle, I thought bad eyes tomorrow, not removing makeup gave me styes. As a teenager, I remember not removing my makeup for a week, gaining super long eyelashes as I added mascara to them each day also gaining three styes by the end of the week. Just this once I would be all right, I hoped, I did not use as much makeup as when I was a teenager.

Chapter Two

In the morning, well no that is wrong, I will start again. In the afternoon, I awoke to an empty house and a note.

"Took Tom home with me I have to sort out 'little line' before he starts chucking his toys at the wall."

I put the kettle on for a pot of tea and another hot water bottle, a doctor's visit on Monday for me.

The phone was ringing, I must say, again, I had heard it during the morning faraway in some place where I was not going to answer it.

'Hello.' I said limply, surprising myself, how bad I sounded.

'I say you all right?' it was Sarah 'I have been trying to get you.'

'Sorry, no I don't feel too good. I have this bladder problem again.'

'Poor you,' she said disinterested, 'it is Sadie, she phoned me from a call box her mobile battery was flat, I have picked her up and brought her home, she is in a bad way, she could barely walk.'

'What did he do to her?' I asked in disgust.

'Yes that was my first thoughts, more like what did "they" do to her. She is not talking much about it but I can hazard a guess.'

'Oh dear Sarah, not nice then, I did not like the look of him.'

'I feel I am to blame, I should have insisted she came home with us, I did take her there and I was the only one sober, what an idiot it was such a nice house and yuppie people, never expected them to treat her like that.'

'Drugs do you think?'

'Defiantly, probably spiked her drinks she won't remember.'

'Where is she now?'

'I put her to bed here. She couldn't go home like that. I collected her kids this morning, her babysitter was throwing a wobbly said she would never sit for her again.'

'I would offer to help but honest love I am not up to it.'

'I can tell by your voice, not to worry, her two kids and my two are amusing themselves arguing. I'll put my ear plugs in,' she often did when her kids started 'hope you feel better, they have the hosepipe out now must go.'

'Bye.' I said to a buzzing phone.

Someone was ringing the doorbell, oh God, Sis is back already and I am not even dressed.

'Coming.' I called as I glanced in the mirror and tried a cheerful face for Tommy's sake.

It was Jonathan, my best friend and Tommy's Godfather.

'Oh it's you.' Not a nice welcome but there you are. He ignored the welcome and my attire. He had a gloomy face doubt if he noticed either what I said or what I look like.

Sitting on the settee sticking his long legs across the room he sighed.

'Something up Johnny?' I enquired staring at him hard, knowing dam well it was her again. Jonathan was married to Diane nice girl but bossy, well to him at least, they had no children, but Jonathan had a son from his first marriage who he sees once a month and usually brings him here, never home to Diane.

Diane was the jealous type, especially about her husband's past. I got on well with her but she could never understand Jonathan's relationship with me. I suppose being truthful, I would say she hated me.

She would not allow him to mention my name in the house or in her company, which by the way is Jenny Roberts, I have not said have I.

He gave another sigh.

'It's her again. Made me sleep on the sofa last night I'm knackered.'

'Want a cuppa?'

'Wouldn't mind.' While waiting for me to produce the tea, he had stretched across the settee, still with his long legs hanging on the floor, he was almost asleep. I pushed the footstool over and put his feet up taking the tea back, I left him there.

'Can you put the telly on?' He mumbled.

'Thought you wanted to sleep?'

'I do, I like sleeping with the telly on.' I did as he asked, there was not much on so I left it as it was, not looking for something pleasing if he was going to sleep through it anyway.

'Football, will that do?'

'Louder.' He requested. Aren't men funny?

All this had woken me up, I had a shower, dressed and woke up some more. I began to make my bedroom tidy, and found my admirers card on the dressing table. A bright attractive card for a bloke I suppose, not business like, no flowers or junk but a cheerful looking thing. Two phone numbers, no address, Peter Martin. Mm, I wonder what he does for a living and how many cards he gave out last night.

Looking out the window, I could see my sister's car backing onto the drive. I opened the door before they rang to come in.

'I won't stop ducks "little line" has to go out and wants the car.'

'Okay Sis.' I called as Tommy came rushing in making for the fridge and anything he could devour while my attention was diverted.

'Oh thanks for last night, sorry I was so late.' I must keep her sweet.

'Was you late, I didn't notice? Bye.' Tuck was waving and blowing me kisses from the back of the car, I returned them.

'Don't go in the front room.' I told Tommy.

'Who's in there the telly is on.' Ignoring me he was in there like a shot then out again.

'What is Uncle Jonathan doing asleep on our sofa?'

'He has been working hard and is tired.'

'Why doesn't he sleep in his own bed?'

'Because Diane has got the decorators in painting their bedroom.' Lies all lies, thought up so quick I would make a good spy.

'Where's Steve?' Jonathan's son.

'Playing football' another lie 'he has a county match today.' Not quite a lie as the clever boy did play football for the county.

'Why can't I play football for the county?' asked Tommy having no idea what that implied or what a county was.

'Because you are not good enough.' He went upstairs then came down again with a football. Taking it into the garden he proceeded to kick it around practicing, bashing it against next door's fence many times. I called from the kitchen window.

'Stop that, keep away from Mr Collin's fence he will not be pleased with you.' Mr Collins was never pleased with Tommy. On nice days, he liked to sleep in his garden and Tommy liked to make loud noises in the garden, waking Mr Collins up.

'Shut up over there.' He would call out and Tommy would come running in.

'He's shouting at me again.' He enjoyed aggravating Mr Collins but was a bit scared of him. When Mr Collins mowed the lawn, Tommy always called out to him.

'Shut up over there.' Fortunately over the sound of his motor mower Mr Collins could not hear. Tommy came into the kitchen with his football.

'How am I going to get good enough for the county if I don't practice?' Chucking the ball down in my way he stomped upstairs.

The phone rang,

'It's me again' said Sarah 'feeling any better, no chance of you popping round?'

'What's wrong with everyone today? I have Jonathan here at the moment asleep on my sofa.'

'Is it her again?'

'Yes afraid so, spending time at his bolt-hole.' Sarah knew Jonathan well, she had been one of his girlfriends before he married his first wife, and he gave her up for the disaster he married. I liked it when they went out together my two best friends becoming one. Through me they had met, not exactly introduced them, just part of the crowd. It was all in the past, best forgotten as it was by Jonathan but not Sarah unfortunately, she still had a fondness for Jonathan, I would say more than she ever has towards anyone else.

Like me, she had never married. Her two kids had two different fathers, neither took any responsibility. They knew they were their kids but had others in other places so admitted to none of them.

My Tommy was conceived in the back of a car. Never laid eyes on the father since.

A posh car I might add, a nice experience from a nice handsome bloke, forgot his name the very next day, then wished I had remembered when I found out I was pregnant.

I remember the car a Mercedes, loads of room in the back, enjoyed ourselves making Tommy I remember that.

Tommy's middle name is Merck, my dad thought that most strange.

'What sort of name is that don't you mean Mark?'

'No Merck MERCK' spelling it out for him.

'Sounds like a cowboy' said mum.

My older sister had a guess and of course

was right. I will tell Tommy one day, hope he enjoys the joke, in between time he thinks he is named after a cowboy.

Getting back to an anxious Sarah still on the telephone.

'Is she okay now?' I asked.

'No that is why I would like you to come round. She has locked herself in the bathroom, has been in there for ages. I knocked on the door but she is not answering, suppose she's slit her wrist?'

'Don't be daft, she is just having a good soak. How are the kids?'

'Arse holes all of them.'

'Don't go into details I'll come round.'

'Oh ta.'

What have I said?

I looked in on Jonathan he was fast asleep, the telly was blaring out. Tidying myself up a bit, and calling out for Tommy to get in the car. I wrote a large note about where I was. Emergency, back soon, and pinned it onto the bottom of his trousers, he would see it there. We went to Sarah's house.

She had not slit her wrists, of course, but was upset big time. When we arrived, she was sitting in the kitchen drinking black coffee and nodding at everything.

No matter what we said to her, she nodded in agreement. I plunged in.

'Do you want to forget what happened or take it further, like reporting the incident and the goings on at that place to the police?'

'Jenny!' Sarah snapped at me in a disapproving tone.

'I don't want to take it further and I can't forget it.'

'No dear of course you can't but forgetting it I mean say nothing, let it pass, keep away from those people and that house, or go to the police as you rightly can?'

'Oh no, oh no.' She was no longer nodding, shaking her head now.

'Okay I take that as no police, just between us, we don't discuss this with anyone.'

'Ruth has just pulled up.' Sarah went to let Ruth in, I told Sadie to cheer up or tell her. She could not cheer up and was not going to be able to do so for at least six months by the look of her.

Ruth was shocked when she the state of Sadie, even more shocked when the story was told with Sadie adding some undesirable bits that she remembered. It did appear to do her good as she told us the "goings on" making her angry, that was better than the depression.

At one time, she wanted to go back to that house and give them a "piece of my mind".

It took us a long while to get her to grasp that it was her own fault and as unpleasant as it was, she was not taken advantage of and stayed with them willingly.

She insisted she took no drugs.

Ruth took her home to go to bed for the rest of the day. I brought her kids home with me.

Mo Lily

Chapter Three

Jonathan was still asleep, I turned the television down a little and looked at these two kids. A cheeky looking, very attractive girl of twelve and a younger boy who did whatever she told him to do, usually mischievous things.

My ten year old fell in love. He gazed at her openly. She kicked him. Great!

'Anyone hungry?'

'Yeah' they all shouted.

'Sit down at the table.' I acted the waiter and went round with a notepad taking their orders.

'Sorry sold out of toad-in-the-hole, their first request. We have eggs and bacon and eggs and baked beans and, eggs, and, and eggs.'

'I don't like eggs.' Sadie's son told me.

Tommy gave me his order.

'Baked beans and bacon and cheese on top.' Only because he has that often.

'Is there any eggs in that?' asked the boy.

'No.'

'I'll have the same.' The twelve-year-old

Lush said but she liked eggs so she would have two eggs put on top, please. She got one egg.

The telly went off and the front room door opened, Jonathan appeared, note in hand.

'That got you up, you could smell the bacon.' I smiled at him.

'It's beans, bacon and cheese Uncle Jonathan.'

'And eggs,' said the Lush.

'Okay fine all that for me ta.'

'And,' I said 'a nice cup of tea.'

'Sounds best of all.' We all ate, I just had enough bacon to go round. While I cleared up they went into the garden and Jonathan played silly games with them. He looked much better than when he came in.

'Going home Jen.'

'Okay mate.'

'Thanks again "bolt-hole" till the next time.'

Jonathan left, all the kids waved him off.

'Where's your dad going?' Asked the Lush.

'He's not my dad silly, he is my Godfather.'

'Your dad is God?' breathed the little boy.

'Don't be stupid' said his sister.

Jonathan had a mum and two sisters he

never went to them, they never helped. Always picked fault and were very nosey.

The children played happily together, the Lush was in control and got her young males running around for her, they were pleased to do as she requested. Tommy certainly was. In five or six years I could see her doing the same with all males, she wouldn't get put into the position her mother was in, neither would I, but who can tell.

I eventually had time to get upstairs to make the beds, it was six o'clock. The kids were watching television. After a good clear up I picked up the card I was given again. He had written on the back.

"In this house of madness there is you, do contact me". Hmm what a smoothie, Martin Peters, turning the card over, oh no it is Peter Martin another, hmm. I tore the card in half and threw it in the bin. What a place it was I am too old for all this.

Sadie's children went home to a mother who with the help of some paracetamol had pulled herself together. In our house we had an early night, I had work tomorrow but would go to the doctors early.

'Yes Mrs Roberts it does appear you may have a bladder infection.' I was started on a course of antibiotics while waiting for a urine test result. Lunchtime I collected my lifesavers at the local chemist viewing what I had in the bag, I bumped into a person.

'Very sorry.'

'Hello.' Said the person, who was it? Oh him old lovely eyes with the cards for everyone.

'Strange places we meet, not ill?' He enquired looking at my little prescription bag that I was trying to stuff into my handbag unnoticed.

'No, but not well.' I managed to say, what sort of comment was that, no, but not well. Who cares?

'Er, are you collecting a prescription?' I asked moving the conversation over to him.

'Going in there.' He pointed to the optician's side of the chemist, 'I broke my glasses, look.' He took them from his pocket, they were snapped clean in half.

'My you have been rough with them.'

'I sat on them.'

'Well yes very rough, careless.' I told him, hark at me sounds like I am talking to Tommy.

He smiled at me, well more a laugh really.

'I shall not be a second just have to hand these in, would you like a coffee?'

'I am on my lunch break.'

'A bite to eat as well then. Stay there!'

He went into the opticians, I may have spoken to him the same way I talk to Tommy but 'stay there' who does he think he is. However, I stayed there.

Taking my elbow, he guided me out of the chemist and into a pub further along the shopping parade. There was a nice smell of food.

'Hi Pete.' A man said, Pete nodded and put me in a seat. Shoved a menu at me and waited.

'Just soup will be fine.' I told him.

'I will have the same, what is it today?'

'Oh er,' taking a better look, 'it is vegetable.'

'Nice, two vegetable soups.' He left me to place the order for our food. I looked around at the chap who had said hello and the other two he was with they looked okay.

The place was nice I had never been in here before. No sooner was he back asking if I wanted a drink when a young girl came over to us with our soups, nice looking soup, rolls and butter. Very appetizing I tucked in, usually a sandwich had to suffice for lunch, eaten at my desk, this was a treat.

'Thank you but I will hold on for a drink. Do you come here every day?' I asked.

'No just the glasses got me out. But I have been here a few times, never disappointed.'

'If there was more time I imagine their meals are good.' Just idle chat to this stranger, I was not getting too friendly, Sadie's experience still fresh in my mind. I would pay for my own soup.

After finishing our soup, which did not take long and was very nice. Peter, that is right not Martin, sat back.

'Strange house Saturday' he said 'well not a strange house, quite a nice house nothing wrong with it, just strange people.'

'Did you think so as well, are they your friends?'

'Good heavens no, I was dragged along as a friend was driving, not my cup of tea at all, I was called a spoilt sport and all those sort of things when I told him I wanted to leave.'

'A bit like me, but we had no idea what it would be like just a party, stuck up toffs with nasty minds.' Stop it Jenny don't get on one.

'I called a taxi after you went and left them to snort their drugs alone.' My eyes widened, no doubt my mouth as well.

'Were they? I didn't see any snorting.'

They started surreptitiously then the more they took the more blasé they became, prats, sorry.' he realized what he had said.

'That's okay I agree prats.' We laughed, his friend looked over at us, wondering who I was, I guess. Peter would fill him in later, how would he describe me to them. He doesn't even know my name. I reached my hand across the table towards him.

'Jenny Roberts by the way, not married, age thirty two, one kid.' Christ almighty why did I say all that. He grinned and shook my hand.

'Er Peter Martin, some say Martin Peters, I don't care I answer to either and a lot worse, not married, well anymore, divorced, no kids, shall not lie thirty-nine.'

He made me giggle. Unfortunately, I had to look at my watch, lunch hour did mean just an hour.

'You have to go?' He enquired 'and no drink, time for a sherry perhaps?'

'No Peter, thanks all the same I must return.'

'Another time perhaps?' He said. As I rummaged in my purse for some money.

'Please no, what would him over there say if he sees you paying for your own soup?' He stood up as I did.

'Please stay.' I told him.

'Bye Jenny, you have my phone number anytime.' He gave me two soft kisses one on each cheek. Made me blush, idiot. I was not sure who was the idiot him or me.

Directly I got home, I poked about in the dustbin looking for his card that I had torn up and discarded. There was half of it, I turned the dustbin upside down to find the other half.

'What you doing Mum?' Asked "himself".

'Just lost something important.' Was it important I wondered as I stuck the two halves back together with Sellotape, giving it a brief wipe clean.

I phoned Sarah that night.

'They were snorting cocaine at that house did you know?'

'I didn't know, how do you know?' I should have guessed she would ask that, I pulled a face grimacing, come on spy get out of this.

'I met someone lunchtime who was there and see more than I did.'

'More than me as well, who is she?' I sighed, ooer, do I tell her? What the hell nothing in it.

I filled Sarah in with the details, starting with the card.

'You kept that a secret.'

'No, not at all, it is no secret I just told you didn't I?'

'What's his name?' I did not want to tell her but it sounded strange not to say.

'Martin, no Peter.'

'Make up your mind ducks or is there two of 'em?'

'No, no, it is Peter.'

'I see.' We said no more as I heard a crash her end of the phone, those kids of hers again. Saved by the crash, she had to go.

I never got to ask how Sadie was, I could always phone her myself but she would depress me. I started preparing our salad tea.

'Rabbit's food.' Tommy told me anything that was not sausages beans or bacon was no good in his eyes.

Later that night the Sellotape stuck to my thumb as I ran it back and forth over Peter

Martin's card staring at the numbers, the landline number was not local, but there was a mobile number I would use that. Would I? Would I use any number, what was I thinking of? I put the card down and went to check on Tommy.

He was partly hanging out of his top bunk bed, I tucked him back into the bed, concerned that he will fall out of it one night. Tomorrow I would dismantle it, why wait until he does fall.

'Thank you Mummy.' He said to me in his sleep as I made him comfortable. I returned to my bedroom to go to bed, took hold of Peter Martins card and tossed it back into the waste paper basket. My little man was my man, there was no room for anyone else.

The next morning I took the thing out of the basket and put it in my underwear draw, not a good place I thought, so took it out and stuffed it between some books on the bookshelf. For Christ's sake I told it as I stuffed it well in.

Chapter Four

Sadie got over her experience and never spoke of it again. Ruth saw her ex-boyfriend Jeff one Friday night. He explained they had many gatecrashers at his party and gosh was his mother upset.

He had her carpets cleaned before she got home, she noticed straight away and a few things went missing or were broken. Yes, it was a daft idea he hoped it would be a nice little gathering but it turned into a free for all.

'My sister is still not talking to me, someone tried it on with her she gave him a black eye, was you there then?'

Thank God, we left when we did.

None of this stopped us from having our nights out.

Sadie soon came back to normal. Ruth who was always hard up and made one drink last all night if some kind sole didn't treat her. She did not care, she had one demanding daughter who took all her money, not because she deserved it more for a peaceful life.

Are you getting the hang of us all? Sarah has two kids, two arsehole kids, she says they don't know how to be kids. They drove her up the wall, now they don't, not because their better but because she ignores them most of the time, oh yes and the ear plugs.

Her home is wrecked, so is her car. I told you about that, not at all good, I do not know how she gets it past the MOT test, sleeps with the bloke probably. Her house and garden are worse. Sometimes she has a bloke home, he never stays as apart from the horrible kids, once he is out of the sack with Sarah he can see jobs to be done. The bathroom door does not close properly, there is no lock, the tap drips "don't open the blind it will fall down on you" and he hasn't got downstairs yet.

I won't talk about the garden I will leave that to your imagination.

Ruth is completely different a small woman with a small house, she is neat and tidy, so is her house. She does not have much but what she has is good. Her car is immaculate, she works for a car show room and has a new car often, we never go out in it, she never takes her turn to drive, she would sooner pay for a taxi. Not that she can afford one, she earns enough money but her high and mighty strumpet of a daughter takes it all.

Jackie is sweet, our matriarch, she lives and cares for her elderly mother so cannot always join us. She has one married son. We all use the same babysitting agency, I use my sister when I can. However, they will not look after elderly mothers. Jackie is put on a spot sometimes and has to decline a night out.

We went out the next Friday just the three of us. Jackie's mum was poorly.

We bumped into a very old friend of mine, Les. We learnt our sex together at a young age, never went out together but did plenty of experimenting. He still does his experimenting whenever he gets a chance, he is not an, on in up and off man, he makes things last as long as you can take it.

Recons he reads the Kama Sutra, load of rubbish he cannot manage to read a newspaper and understand it. Just ideas he gets, some are good ideas others downright disgusting, like the time with the curry sauce. I've still got the stain on my mattress to prove it and a blob on my silk headboard where he managed to wave it about, I won't explain what he was waving or why, but you can guess.

'Going home alone?' He asked me.
'Not now you've asked I suppose.'
'Good on yer love, don't leave without me.'
'Don't get drunk.'
'What me, no way, I can't get a hard on if I'm drunk.'

Arriving home with Les, he quietly went upstairs two at a time, while I paid the sleeping baby sitter.

'He's been fine.' She told me, 'not a sound, thanks for the chocolates.' I was about to say take them with you when I noticed the large box was empty, she had devoured the lot. It pays to keep them happy.

I checked on Tommy, so had Les, fast asleep in the bottom half of his bunk, the rest of the bed in the garage. I spent time in the bathroom, found Les a new toothbrush to use, he was stripped to the waist waiting for me.

'Ta love.' He said taking the toothbrush from me. He returned from the bathroom with his erection poking out through his trousers fly for me to look at.

'See not drunk.' He told me proudly.

'Have you washed it?'

'Thoroughly.' Locking the door, and removing all his clothing wearing nothing except a large erection, he started to blow up a pink balloon.

'You will like this one, you'll see, and it's pink especially for you.' He jumped in bed with me bringing the pink balloon with him.

'Who do you save the blue ones for the blokes?' He banged me on the head with it. The balloon I mean.

I did see, not bad, put this leg here and that one there, shoving his knee between my right leg and hand. I did at one time wonder if I was going to break a bone or get stuck at least.

'Now put your hands like this.' He demonstrated. Wherever did he get these ideas from, off the internet I guessed.

We had fun, at one time he had to put his

hand over my mouth in case I woke Tommy up, I was laughing so much. We were right under the covers good job too, the balloon playing a huge part in our ludicrous antics.

The balloon burst, I screamed with laughter.

None of my friends understand how Les and I are still mates, nothing more than that. Especially Jonathan, he really gets on one.

'You've had Les round here again.'

'So bloody what.' I tell him.

'He's a sex machine.'

'Yes too true he is.'

'You've got no respect for your body.' Jonathan tells me with disgust.

'Yes I have, so has Les, don't fret yourself he doesn't force me to do anything I don't want to, it is enjoyable fun.'

Cor doesn't he moan. He has known Les as long as I have and hears his boasting no doubt. I don't care he gives me a much needed shag once in a while, so what!

Chapter Five

Tommy came in from the garden crying, he was wet and filthy holding places that hurt.

'Whatever happened to you?' I rushed to his aid, looking at sore hands and knees.

'You fell out of that tree didn't you? I told you not to climb up there anymore, you are lucky you have not broken something.'

We had a large oak tree at the end of our garden, very tempting for a young boy and very easy to climb as he often does.

'I didn't fall, he pushed me.'

'Who pushed you there is no one there?'

'Mr Collins.'

'He wouldn't come in our garden.'

'His water did.' I frowned at the sobbing child who was inspecting his sore places.

'And here.' He said pointing to his bottom. I turned him round to inspect and pulled his trousers down, oh a big bruise looming there.

'What water did?' As I could not

understand what he meant.

'The water in the hosepipe.' I get it now, old Collins squirted him with the hose.

'Why would he do that, what was you doing?'

'Just this.' He put his thumbs to his temples waggling his fingers and poked out his huge long tongue that he would find very useful one day, make up for his weeny pecker.

The sobbing stopped.

'You did ask for it that is very rude, thought you were safe up there didn't you?' Nonetheless, it was a stupid thing for a grown man to do, knock a child out of a tree, he could have a broken his back, a wheelchair for life, tubes and oxygen all came to mind. Attending to my son, I got cross with old Collins.

'Go and lay down on your bed until the soreness wears off.' I told Tommy after applying cream and taking another look at his bottom. Cross, I say I was, with the stupid old sod next door, I marched into his garden to have a not so nice a word with him.

Our two back gates were adjoining, there he was the git, still watering the end of his garden. The water tap was near the house, I turned it off. He didn't look up at me he looked at the spray, as you do, thinking it had stopped working he fiddled with it taking a good look. I put the water back on full force. He got soaked with his own water, he shouted something as he saw me, I could not hear what. He threw the hose to the ground it started to snake around out of control, soaking him again, he tried to catch hold of it but failed. I shouted words to him that he could not hear either, but made me feel better just saying them.

As I returned through my gate, I could see my injured son watching from his bedroom window, cheering and making more faces.

Gosh, the bruise did get big, Tommy showed it to everyone, dropping his pants to do so, causing many gasps, and he told them how he could have broken his back. He showed his teacher and got into trouble for flashing his arse in the classroom. The teacher was not at all impressed or concerned with the bruise especially when Tommy said he might not be able to sit at his desk all day.

'You can stand up when it hurts.' Not what

Tommy had in mind, sent home would be better, so he sat on his jumper for comfort.

The girls tittered and asked to see his bum again at playtime.

'Shall I kiss it better?'

'Go on then.'

'Shall I kick it make it bigger?'

Oh Mr Collins what did you stir up?

Another day Tommy accidentally kicked his wonderful football over Mr Collins fence. I didn't see it go, but I did see it come back.

Tommy dragged around the place very sorry he had kicked his ball in that direction wondering if he would ever see it again.

'No you can't knock on his door for it. There it is now, he has thrown it back.' I knew not all was well, it just flopped, no bounce. Tommy ran to get his ball, pleased it was returned, until he sees the puncture hole made with a sharp instrument.

Right git-face I will show you.

'Get in the car Tommy.'

We went to the toyshop to buy another ball. Tommy pulled so many balls out of the large basket container trying to find another the same. I left him to it and wandered off, for ten minutes, I could hear the assistant moaning at him as he tried to explain that this was the best football in the shop. I returned to help the poor man, an unusual thing for me to do.

'What about this one?' I suggested.

'Nope.'

'This one?'

'Not bad. It's like that but different.' He told the salesman.

'This is our most popular one.' He lied just to get rid of us.

'Is it?' Tommy took a better look and believed him.

'We will take it.' I said getting fed up now 'and this one' I stuffed it at him 'and this one.'

'It's got pink on it Mum.'

'Okay, not that one.' I said snatching it back and chucked it into the ball basket.

'This one?'

'Yeah.' The man was trying to hold five footballs now not making a very good job of it, dropping some.

'How many do you need madam?' Loads I told him.

'Make it half a dozen, no say ten or twelve.' Tommy could not believe it, grabbing one back and changing it for a better one. If ever you want to make a young boy happy, buy him half a dozen footballs, or more, all at once. A huge bag was found for the balls and Tommy dragged ten balls to the car, clutching them on the rear seat, I could not see him.

When we got home I found some paint. On Mr Collins fence I painted a target with a red bull's-eye.

'GO' I told to Tommy, 'and if one goes over it doesn't matter, if they all go over, you are not getting any more.'

I stomped indoors, that will show the git. Funny how the noise your own kids make is not half as bad as the noise when they are not yours. I could hear the balls banging on the fence, I thought, 'Good!'

Mr Collins was old, and was always grumpy, Mrs Collins long gone. He was an old git to everyone. The day I opened my front door to the knocking on the glass I wondered, why me?

There was Mr Collins holding his chest in great pain, he came in and collapsed in my hallway. He was having a heart attack, as I tried to loosen his clothing around his throat I called for Tommy to phone the emergency line. He was unconscious now, I grabbed the phone off Tommy and explained the situation.

I understand he died in the ambulance on the way to the hospital.

Tragic, but still an old git.

After several weeks, Tommy was bored in the garden without anyone to annoy. He found no fun in kicking the balls against the fence without being shouted at.

Then they arrived, our new neighbours. A family of them, Rosemarie and Trevor Hopkins, they had two girls, one the same age as Tommy, in his class at school, he was pleased to say. He took her to school every day and fell in love again, big time. Samantha, Sam to most and little Molly the sort of sister that was always "telling mum". I was a young sister but never in the world would I split on my big sister, not even today.

Sam and Tommy were inseparable she was to be my daughter-in-law until she became seventeen when she broke Tommy's heart. She found her Neil and forgot all the Tommy years. I could have brained her for all the upset and misery she brought to our house.

Their parents were fine, except they liked to argue, with each other I mean. Not to me or anyone else, they were nice neighbours. But did they row, anytime, all the time, seemed to thrive on it, noisy arguments in the middle of the night if necessary. Likewise noisy lovemaking. In the summer when the windows were open, it was heard by all. Rosemarie, squealing with delight she was very vocal while having sex, she told Trevor, not quietly, where and how to do it.

I had to keep Tommy's windows shut or he would hear all sorts. When Tommy and Sam became teenagers, I wondered if they were experimenting like me and Les had done. In fear of this, I kept an eye on my son and told Rose to do the same.

Strange I enjoyed it why shouldn't he.

Chapter Six

We managed a Friday night out, all of us. Jackie's brother had taken their mum back to Chelmsford where he lives, for a few days, so we made the most of it for her sake. In addition, maybe Saturday night as well.

We went to the Barley Corn, not a raving place, somewhere quiet where we could sit and chat, we had much catching up to do. Comfortably we settled, quietly laughing, enjoying each other's company, no young kids or old mums to interrupt.

Half an hour into our evening, I looked up to the voice standing next to me.

'Jenny.' It was Peter Martin. We stopped talking and all looked in his direction.

'Hello Peter.' I said, acting cool, no introduction to my friends.

'You never telephoned.' He directed at me intently. All eyes turned to me. She didn't telephone.

'No I forgot.' Lying again. Putting his head on one side, he held his hand out for mine.

'I will have to show you how to remember.' As I took his hand and let him lead me into the garden, he nodded at my companions, who giggled to each other.

Leading me outside and towards the back, he gently pushed me against the wall putting one hand on the wall just above my head and the other around my waist he drew me towards him. Sucking my bottom lip into his mouth, then the top one, letting go he ran his tongue over them.

I stood still with my outspread hands pressed against the wall. He then slowly started to kiss me, snog me with a light passion that I didn't want to end.

Eventually coming up for air, without talking he took me back inside putting me in my seat leaning over he whispered.

'I've wanted to do that since I first saw you.' Then moved back to his friends at the bar.

'Who the devil was that?' asked Sadie.

'I have seen him before somewhere' said Jackie. Sarah grinned and knew.

'Not bad, would one say a smoothie?'

'Yes I guess one would.' I replied as I looked in his direction again. He had his back to me.

Soon forgotten we continued our conversation mainly about Sarah's rotten kids.

A young lad in a long por

t man's apron just his big feet sticking out at the bottom came over to me with a drink.

'Him at the bar sent you this, he said to say.' looking up at the ceiling making sure, he got it right 'you never did have your sherry.'

I took it, I don't think I have ever had a sherry before, only the stuff I put in the Christmas cake. I had a sniff and a taste, it was nice not at all like cooking sherry.

'Sherry?' they all said.

'Yes it's a long story.' I was not going to tell them right now.

'Let's have a taste.' They all took a sip, giving me back half a glass full, the consensus was they liked it.

'The type of drink you have with a meal, my mother likes a sherry.'

Oh God that has really typed me, I looked over to thank him but he and his friends had gone. I lay in bed that night fingering the lips he had sucked. Where did I put his card?

I knew dam well where I had put it, next morning I pulled all the books off the shelf, flicking through the pages shaking them on to the bed, no card. I know I put it there, pushing and shoving books around, looking on the floor and under the bed, no card.

Wiping my hands along the shelf I found it squashed and crumpled at the back sticking down under the wooden shelf.

What a mess it was in, torn in half, stuck back together, now crumpled almost beyond recognition. I could barely read the telephone numbers that I was not going to phone, or was I? No not at all, or I would have already done so.

I put it and the books back, stuffing it well in again in case it crept out.

Chapter Seven

I had another Jonathan day, Saturday lunch time he arrived drunk, unusual for him and driving his car. Which he had abandoned outside my house, a good two feet from the curb and not at all straight.

He fell in the door moaning about the bitch, bad words thrown in. Tommy heard it all, the more I told Jonathan to be quiet the loader he got with his bad words.

'Go to sleep Johnny.' I pushed him down on the sofa and put the television on, the sound up high, and left him, sneaking a bowl close by him just in case he was sick, not getting drunk often it was possible.

An hour later Sarah arrived, we were taking the kids shopping for school uniforms. Upon hearing the noisy telly, she guessed.

'Asleep again is he? She's a cow to him.'

'She's a witch.' Tommy joined in.

'Don't say things like that.'

'She is Uncle Jonathan is buying her a broomstick he told me a big one because she is a big old witch.'

'Have you seen how he has parked his car, never drunk is he?' asked Sarah.

'I'm afraid so.'

'Park his car properly love don't leave it like that sticking out it is bound to get knocked.'

'I'm not moving the great thing it will have to stay there.' Jonathan drove a very large car.

'Give us the keys I will do it.' I shrugged my shoulders at keys, we both thought together, they must be in his pocket. We crept in the front room, no need the television was on so loud he could not hear us. We pulled his body this way and that until we laid hands on the car keys, I didn't miss Sarah groping about in his trousers for more than just the keys.

She in no time parked the car properly. We replaced the keys and made him comfortable, he did not stir. Sarah leant over him and gave his neck a longer than normal kiss.

Back in the kitchen, I looked at her.

'You still love him don't you?' She heaved a great sigh and gazed at nothing wistfully.

'Could say that I suppose much more than those pigs who gave me their arsehole kids.'

'Sarah!'

This was Sarah's way of defending her kids, she did love them but they were such buggers she prepared people before hand and they usually told her what she liked to hear.

'They are not that bad.' If she told them what adorable little creatures they were, which she really hoped they were, people would soon enlighten her with a slur.

This is how she got by at their school.

'Don't give up on them Mrs Hutchinson.'

'MISS Sarah Hutchinson.' Teachers cannot remember everything.

'We will do our best you may be pleasantly surprised, just let us do our job.'

She would come out of the parent's evening delighted.

'Going to do their job, too true they are, I'm not a teacher, I'm a mother, the one who breast feeds.'

However, they were naughty, I could never manage them for more than an hour at a time and they did not do Tommy any good.

It took him a week to get back to normal and to stop saying "No" and "I want". They were not at all alike, different dads, I told you. But they were both big, you had to join in with them or risk a heavy thump.

Two girls, you didn't think that did you. They sound like naughty boys, somehow it is worse when it is bad girls, we do not expect our girls to be bad do we, little madams with catty tongues maybe, but these two were vicious, crafty manipulating, lazy and as Sarah says both of them an arsehole.

Good job Sarah was tough, the way they spoke to her at times, you are not supposed to hit your kids but Sarah does. I have seen a good right-hander strike home many a time. And a fist, good job they can duck quickly.

In the car, it is murder, well not quite, but one day maybe, as she drives Sarah will deliver her back handers across the child's mouth without a pause in her fast driving.

She has often kicked the child out of the car to find its own way home.

They never learn, one day they will see all that gob gets them nowhere.

The eldest one, many years later, did

blossom, boys did it.

She got herself a paper round. Sarah had to yank her out of bed to do it, but do it she did.

Grabbing her first month's salary she went straight to the hairdressers and had her hair dyed red. She had to work another month to afford the stud in her nose that she wanted.

Sarah hit the ceiling, promised to cut it all off, she would sooner a bald daughter than that mess.

'It's not bad Sare, it was done nice. She could have had done it herself and made a right cockup.' I told her.

'She should have asked me first.' Oh so that was what it was all about, losing control.

Boys came next, her mouth turned sweet.

'Didn't know she knew nice' said her mum 'bet she's dropping her draws already.'

'Sarah stop it she is still a little girl.'

What did I know, when she asked her mum could she go on the pill, Sarah couldn't get her to the doctor quick enough.

'Not that I am doing anything Mummy it is just in case, I must be prepared.'

'Christ this is worse than bad,' she told me 'makes me feel old. Bet she is getting more than I am' moaned Sarah.

Back to the present, Sarah took another look in the front room at Jonathan.

'His son is lovely isn't he, and clever?'

'Yes a clever boy all right.'

'If he had stayed with me he could have been my son.'

'Stop it Sarah it is past, life has moved on it is how it is.'

'Yes you are right.' Cheering up very quickly she turned the conversation to last night and Peter Martin. This I did not want. The muddled place in my head where he was did not need stirring up.

'You still got the card he gave you?'

'No-o' I slowly said.

'You have I can tell, show me.'

'Definitely not, I don't want to talk about him, who the devil is he anyway? Who does he think he is?'

'Touchy.' Was all Sarah said to this giving me a look. Jonathan appeared.

'I am leaving my bolt-hole for a far, far better place.' Spreading his arm in a dramatic gesture, as he still held on the door handle with the other hand to steady himself.

'You bloody well are not, you are over the limit, get back in your hole and sleep some more.' I shouted at him with determination.

'I'm hungry.'

'I will feed you, get comfy on the settee.'

'I need a slash.'

'Go and do it then.' I made him some cheese on toast, I was not going to make a fuss. He did eat it in the kitchen with us and drank the tea I also made. He went to the toilet again and disappeared back into the front room.

Sarah left reminding me we are going out that night again.

Oh yes, I had forgot, two nights running, tonight would be a rave up a different type of place, too many drinks and much dancing, home late.

Just before Sis arrived to baby sit, again I poked Jonathan.

'Johnny I am going out tonight, my sister is coming round soon you have to go home, I will take you.' He woke up quickly,

'No you can't do that she will go mental if she sees you.'

Great, nice to know how others think of you.

'I can drive look,' holding his hands out to

show me 'steady as a rock I will be fine.'

'Okay love, go straight home won't you.'

'Yeah, yeah bye ducks.' He went off tooting and yelling 'Ta' out of his window.

We were going to the King's Crown pub a nice place, always packed, you could never get a seat, come to think of it, I don't think there are any. Loud music played by a right berk who talked over the music a lot, so distorted you had no idea what he was saying.

Everyone danced or wiggled on the spot. Friendly crowd, you felt a bit like meat as the blokes eyed you up and down, so we did the same back.

By the end of the evening to have had a goodnight, you had to find someone to go home with. Taking stock of the drinkers, I have to admit I feel a bit old, not older than the blokes, but older than the young made up tarts, could even be school kids, that were hanging round the bar.

Tony came over to me, I didn't know him but that was his name.

'I am fed up with chatting to these kids that have just left school or still go to school, have you seen the age of some of them?.' That was his opening chat up line.

'So you looked around for a grannie?'

'You're not a grannie are you?' he asked.

'Just a joke but I am a mum and legal.'

'That sounds better. I'm Tony.' He introduced himself. Jenny I said in reply.

'It should be reported serving under age kids, under age for sex as well, could get you into all sorts of trouble.'

'Are you a grandad?' I asked him.

'Of course not I wouldn't be in this place if I was, why do you ask do I look like one?'

'No but you sound like one.'

'Let's start again, Hi Jenny, let me buy you a drink.' He politely suggested.

'Thanks but it will take you ages to get served, a Southern Comfort if you see a gap, but don't make an effort, I have enough look.' I held my glass up to show him, it was nice to be asked by a stranger I thought.

I did not realise for a long while, I had left the girls and kept in Tony's company for ages. We got on well, both of us moaning and putting the world to right between us. Agreeing with most of the wrongs and our dislikes and finding new ones to bring to each other's attention. Making notes of the kids at the bar, their mannerisms and how they were dressed, where their hands went while getting friendly with some poor bloke, or maybe lucky bloke. We did eventually see the funny side of it and managed to laugh. And he bought me a drink.

We had a good night, must have, as he came home with me. We had sex, that was the idea after all, quietly as I explained my sister and our sons were in the other rooms.

He was nice and gentle but a bit quick, my only complaint. He left early before everyone got up. With a see you next week promise. I did not tell him I don't get out that regular.

Before the morning had gone half way, there was Sarah.

'You liked him didn't you?'

'He was sweet, that's about it.'

'What does he do for a living?'

'I don't know.'

'It does make a difference if you are going to get involved with someone.' Sarah always being one to suss out the money first.

'I shan't be getting involved at all.'

'Not that sweet then. You like the sherry man best don't you?'

'Do not, don't like anyone.' I miserably told her.

Today was Sunday, a funny day I always thought, definitely for churchgoers, but not much good to anyone else.

I never enjoy Sunday as a day because I was always getting ready for Monday.

After all the preparation, school uniform in order for the week, shirts ironed my working clothes sorted and ready to wear. Sunday lunch eaten always late, never lunch time.

Tommy was out with some scruff he had befriended, I lay on the bed for half hours rest. Looking at the shelf of books, thinking what was hidden there. I ran my fingers over the lips he sucked again remembering.

To hell with it, I pulled the books out and found his card, easy to find this time, conveniently placed for when it would be wanted. Hard to make out the numbers it is in such a crumpled state, was that a three or a five? I would use the land line as my numbers are withheld on that. Heaven forbid he should find that out, why?

Mm, not a local code, wonder where he lives? I dialed his land line.

'Hello' he said after just two rings. Oh God its him, I said nothing. Then he said in an off putting, slow Dracula type voice.

'*Speak to me.*' I hung up. What a state to get in, can't do that again. I looked up the out of town area code, it was Windsor. Blimey posh.

Why did he come our way so often? He liked slumming it, no we don't live in the slums, just Essex, not as good as Windsor.

I started to wash the dinner dishes. Thinking truthfully about this Peter Martin, forgetting the stupid kiss he mesmerized me with what else did I know about him.

Lovely eyes, oh yes must not forget them, the rest of him nice, not short of a bob or two by the look of him, that would please Sarah, money first.

He lives in Windsor, well his land line does. Comes to Essex often, how often, let me see, maybe monthly, always stays, he hasn't time to get back to Windsor.

I have seen him Saturday into Sunday night,

then Monday when he sat on his glasses. So not just a weekend visit, then again on a Friday. Well he must work here on and off. I had finished washing up and returned to the book shelf.

I know he is there in Windsor, sitting near the telephone as he answered quick enough.

To hell with it I used my mobile this time, that would give him my number.

'Hello.'

'Hi it's me Jenny.' Oh done it, I was going to hyperventilate, I sat down.

'Hello there, how are you?'

'Yes, fine, I was just clearing out and found your card thought I would give your number a ring before I chucked it out.'

'Don't do that Jenny I would only have to give you another.' I felt awkward now.

'One is sufficient, I said I was clearing out.'

'Okay point taken.' We went on to chat almost about anything and nothing for ages. He did come to Essex about once a month. Told you I'd make a good spy. He would contact me before his next visit and we would make arrangements from there.

'I'll give you my number.' I stupidly said.

'No need I have it showing here, I will just

put Jenny next to it.' Silly me of course he has. Not to let him know I had looked up his code.

'Where are you now?' Sounding interested.

'Just outside Windsor.'

'Windsor nice place.' I casually said, 'I have never been there but the Queen goes there that's good enough for me.' He laughed but it was more like a titter.

'Okay Peter see you again when you are this way.'

'Goodbye Jenny, thanks for phoning.' We both hung up our receivers at the same time. I felt hot, shall I phone Sarah? No keep it a secret for a while nothing may come of it.

That night as I drifted off to sleep, I heard my mobile buzz, I had a message "Goodnight Jenny" wow I did not know how to take that as my breath quickened. I decided not to send an answer. Every night I got the same message, always ignored by me, a bit bitchy or rude, no mysterious.

Chapter Eight

Next weekend I met Jacob, Cor blimey did I meet Jacob, no Les anywhere. I didn't have sex with Jacob but he did come home with me.

Tommy was staying at my sister's house as "little line" was working away. We could romp around the house naked, but didn't.

'Hope you haven't brought me home for sex, because I am not that keen.'

'What not keen on me?'

'No not you, just not into sex much, overrated and hard work, so I don't indulge.'

'How old are you?' I asked he didn't tell me.

'What you got to eat? Can you play cards?'

I found some basic food for us to consume and he produced a pack of cards, my phone buzzed with its goodnight message, if he only knew what I was up too. We played easy card games then Jacob showed me how to play Kalookie, strange and difficult I eventually got the hang of it, good enough to pass for him but nowhere near good enough for the tournaments he told me about that he entered at the casinos.

It was absorbing and intrigued me, dawn was breaking as I made some toast, we had played cards all night. After the toast I told him, and it was true.

'I think I am tired.'

'I had best go.'

'You can sleep here.' I pointed to Jonathan's sofa.

'Thanks love but there is a game at the casino this afternoon I want to be there.'

'What with no sleep?'

'I will pop something to keep me awake.'

'I see.' I said pulling a face. He called a taxi and left.

Another phone call from Sarah, we had a laugh telling her about my experience. Tommy came home, I was shattered and went to bed early.

A couple of weeks, a phone call followed by a meeting.

It was Peter, he took me for a meal, very nice. I will not bore you with the details, he treated me kindly, polite, full of confidence, you can imagine. He didn't come in, no shag, just a quick peck goodnight not even a hug or better still a grope, I think I was disappointed.

The next day an early phone call.

'Did you sleep well?'

'I did thank you.'

'I have to pop home there is something I have forgotten do you fancy a drive?'

'Well there is Tommy.'

'Bring him he will like it there.'

'No I'll see what I can arrange, what time?'

'As soon as you can, ring me when you are ready.'

'Sarah, you must help me!' She took Tommy for as long as you like, she told me I was to enjoy myself and not worry. She is a good mate.

Driving to Windsor, Sunday morning was nice, his car was super, as I knew it would be. We did not talk much.

'Not far now.'

'Is that the castle?' I asked as it came into view.

'Yes have you not seen it before?'

'No, you don't live there do you?' As we

seemed to be making straight for it.

'No thanks.' He said.

'Peter?' I said in an enquiring tone.

'Yes.' He answered wondering what I was going to say no doubt.

'What do you do for a living?' I had to ask for Sarah's sake, then immediately felt I was being rude.

'I will show you.' Crikey, what is he going to show me? Shortly we stopped in a quiet road, empty but full of offices.

'Over there.' He said pointing to a large building on the corner all tinted glass with many windows. Along the front in blue, it said Martin Merchants, in gold leaf on each window, it said the same but smaller, a large building with several floors, large glass doors at the entrance.

'Oh.' I said as the penny dropped, Peter Martin, Martin Merchants.

'Do you want to look inside?'

'No, no that's all right.' Phew, I sat back as he started the engine again.

He had a nice house, of course, not too big but not small like mine. Well cared for, immaculate really, oldish, not modern I mean. He showed me around the house, he called out to the kitchen, "only me" and took me upstairs, fantastic views from each window.

'This is my room.'

'I thought they were all your rooms?' I cockily said.

'Well yes, but this is the one I use.'

'I see.' He touched me as I looked out the window, turned me round to face him, then that kiss again. I don't remember how I got to lay on the bed, or when he locked the door.

My clothes peeled off as did his, not ripped off. We slipped under the bedspread cover and had the most divine sex, this was not sex, it was making love, gentle and sweet.

I am not short of sex as you know but I had not had it like this for a long while, if ever.

We lay together afterwards both relieved, glad the ice breaking first time was over.

Peter fingered the little dip we have in our necks just below the Adams apple, we all have one, bet you are touching yours now. I expect it has a name that none of us know. He rubbed his finger round and round this place while we talked, then the finger moved towards other places, again he took me, I let him.

Wandering hand in hand over lawns and beside flowerbeds, walking through an arch we came upon a large pond. We sat on a wooden seat looking at the many fish.

'My dad built that,' pointing to the pond, 'did it himself, would not let the gardener help, it is called Charlie's Puddle.'

'Some puddle.' Did it himself, it was huge.

'Did he use machinery?'

'No dug it out by hand alone, started for scratch. As most things dad did, alone from scratch, I inherited the business from him, he trained me well, starting when I was about twelve. And the house, I was born there.'

'Lovely what a life and mum?' I enquired.

'Oh she is still with us, she lives in Kent, left this place as soon as dad died. She moved "up market and modern" she tells everyone, but we will be the judge of that, maybe modern but do not know where she gets the up market from. She never comes back here. No wish too is all she says.

'Let's get some lunch it is getting late, do you like fish?'

'I do.'

'The Fisherman it is then, it's not far, I must

collect the stuff I came for.' We had a late lunch in a very nice pub, come restaurant, Peter called out "I'm off now" to the kitchen as we left the house, there was still no response from the kitchen Peter appeared not to expect any.

Driving back after changing gear he put his hand on my knee, and then back again after the next gear change. I am not sure what I was making of that. He dropped me off, not coming in again and rushed off with his box of papers.

I phoned Sarah.

'Wow Sare.' I said as she answered her phone.

'You've had sex with him haven't you?' was her first response. I ignoring her, enquired.

'How's Tommy?'

'Well he is off the conservatory roof now, that is where they have been most of the day, even had lunch up there.'

'Sounds like you encouraged them.' I ungratefully said imagining her lumps of kids pushing my Tommy off the roof.

'Not at all they were good for a change.'

'What were they doing up there for such a long time?'

'I have no idea, looking at each other's parts probably.'

'Sarah!'

Tommy never enlightened me when I asked what they did on the roof.

'Nothing much.' Perhaps Sarah was right about that after all.

I got another text, Peter does not appear to make phone calls at all, well never to me, just a short text. A bit more information this time.

"I am returning to Windsor this evening for a while, I will text you when I shall be here again." No hello, goodbye, thank you or kiss your arse, I ignored it.

Lunchtime Monday I walked around town near a large shoe shop, I am sure I had seen it before, Martin Merchants, being of no interest to me I had not paid it much attention.

A big place, blue and glass, tinted glass so I could not see inside properly. Knowing he was in Windsor I pressed my nose to the glass and still couldn't see much. Someone came out the door and held it open for me, so I went in.

A vast, open reception area, with a prim looking girl sitting at a desk, further over from the door. There were some leaflets on display, I started showing interest in them.

'May I help you?' The girl said in a stuck up manner, looking down on me, I could tell.

'Is Mr Peter Martin available?' She was somewhat surprised I was enquiring after her boss. She was afraid he was not available but she would get someone else who could deal with me. I wasn't going to be dealt with, so grabbing a few leaflets I told her not to worry only Mr Martin would do.

'I will call another time.' I left her looking me up and down with suspicion.

I work in a small solicitor's office, excellent pay for the little I do. I can turn my hand to anything from writing his letters, answering the phone calls and making the sweet tea, he likes. He thinks I am an angel and cannot do without me, he possibly can't.

Buying a cress sandwich and a cream cake, I returned to my desk early to read the Martin Merchant leaflets. Something to do with shipping, hard to understand and looked boring. He certainly made plenty of money doing it. Perhaps they export arms to undesirable foreign countries, crooked stuff against the law. I am acting the spy again.

That was wicked thoughts, sorry Peter.

He was still a mystery he made a huge amount by the looks of it, why was he at all interested in me, a single mum, and way out of his class. He would be better suited to some stuck up floozy from a good background, with enough money to match his own. This was just a game for him, I would jog along for the fun of it.

I got my late text when I was in bed I waited for it. "Goodnight sleep tight" oh another word. I ignored it.

Chapter Nine

The unexpected happened, Jackie's mother died while still staying with her son. Jackie was most upset, although her mum was old, she did not expect it to happen. It took her a long while to adjust, living alone she wasn't keen on it. Her married son called to see her often as we did but as we had little kids and Jackie didn't, it was awkward.

Tommy moaned and we never stayed long. She was able to come out with us anytime now, all the time if she had her way.

Us not always affording to go out, buying something new to wear, getting our hair done and paying a baby sitter, all before you paid for a drink or two.

Besides, we were often tired with the kids to look after. Jackie had none of this so found herself a new friend, Bart. He was nice, we all agreed, they suited each other.

Mason Bartholomew what a lovely name, just known as Bart. I bet Peter Martin would like a name like it. Wasted on Bart, as he was a plumber. Jackie said she didn't like being alone and by God she wasn't for long, Bart moved in with her.

He wanted to come out with us on our girl's nights, we put our foot down, refusing him.

Jackie always left early "must get home to Bart" I hope it lasts for her.

Ruth was next a plain old Fred, nice enough bloke, but her daughter hated him. Attention went from her and mummy spent the money on herself. The relationship was doomed.

Her spoilt daughter did her best to upset Fred. In turn, he could not stand her. They tried and he had to admit everything was perfect about Ruth and perhaps when her daughter was older and offhand they would get back together.

They parted friends. Ruth heard that within six months he had married a woman with no kids.

'I should have stayed with Jeff and helped him spend his money.' Party Jeff remember.

I don't think there was a hope in hell of anyone doing that and I am sure she did not have the opportunity to stay, he dropped her soon losing interest as he does with them all. He is looking for Miss or Mrs Right, someone with more money than him preferred.

Sarah, well as you know still carries the flag for our Jonathan, she meets different people but with her kids and her tongue in cheek attitude she has to anyone else they soon leave her. I think she has resigned herself to the fact that for her there is no other person than Johnny and does not bother getting acquainted with anyone else.

Me you know my position. One thing I had not bargained for Peter wanted to meet Tommy. Dreading this as judging by other friends once they meet your offspring the relationship is doomed.

'Whatever for?' I asked Peter after his request to meet my son.

'I like little boys.'

'What is the matter with little girls?' Thinking of a couple of little girls that had a lot wrong with them.

'I like them as well.'

'You fancy a kid's time, getting back to your

youth meeting them at their level or just being nosey?' I quizzed him not thinking it was necessary for him to meet Tommy and what would Tommy's reaction be.

'I had no youth Jenny, I told you dad started training me for the business at a very early age, there was no time for youthful activities.'

'And you want kid's company now to do this, football and all that running around.'

'Yes sounds great, I'm no good at football at all but I like to try.'

'That will please Tommy neither is he, and everyone else is good making him look worse. He will love it if he is better than you.'

'That is settled, we go out Saturday, or Sunday it is up to you?'

'Saturday, Sunday is always a getting ready for school day.'

'Is he any good at school, I can teach him advanced maths.'

'No way, do you want to make an enemy before you have met? Stick to football.'

'Fine we will take a trip out, have lunch somewhere nice then find somewhere to go mad.'

'Going mad are you, don't expect me to join

in with you.' I did wonder if this was going to be too much for Tommy, just met then spending all day with a stranger, supposing he hated him on sight.

I need not have worried. They shyly met both a little shy I would say. Then Tommy with many 'wows' jumped into the back of his car with delight, Peter was a winner from that moment.

Food, 'have what you want' Peter told him. What a load of junk food Tommy managed to devour. Then a game of football, his kicking and running left Tommy in hysterics as Peter was useless at both.

Collapsing next to me both out of breath, hot and thirsty from playing awful football.

'Are you good at anything?' I asked he raised one eyebrow, oh very cute with those long eyelashes.

'You need to ask?'

'You know what I mean.'

'I'm good at squash.'

'Squashing what?' asked Tommy

'Don't go any further' I said to Peter, 'it's a game that oversized men play to keep fit.' None the wiser Tommy shut up.

It was time for a drink and soon time to go

home, Peter came in, Tommy gave him a guided tour of my mean pad. Including "that is Jonathan's sofa", be dammed it is not, I winced as he mentioned Jonathan.

Upstairs all Tommy's collection of special things came out for his new friend to admire. Showing great interest, politely, I thought and tried to interrupt bringing it to an end and for my trouble, they told me to "Shh" by Peter and "Go away Mum" from my son.

We had coffee and cake in the garden, nice. My garden is nice in the parts that Tommy is not allowed to play, not my doing, I have a gardener.

'Can you swim?' Peter asked Tommy

'Yes I am good at it, Mum can't swim at all, she is useless.'

'Really can't swim?' he said looking at me as if it was some sort of disability, like can't talk or something.

'Shall we go tomorrow?'

'Tomorrow?' I disputed.

'Yes we can go? You get the things ready for school.' Peter told me, more like ordered me.

'But I don't go to school it's him that has to

get ready.' I objected somewhat displeased.

'Like what?' said Tommy

'Well there's uniform and homework, polish your shoes and bed early.'

'Done my homework and you do the rest.'

'Well you have to go to bed early.'

'We will be back way before bedtime and I am sure he will sleep well.' Peter was looking at Tommy telling me, not asking, with Tommy nodding in agreement.

That night we made love in my bed, notice I called it love, he was right he was good at something. Too dam good, I felt intoxicated, he kissed every part of me and I in return felt the need to do the same to him. Using my mouth is not something I normally indulge in but I wanted too with this man and I did.

Awake half the night playing our games and talking. I asked him a question that mystified me.

'Why did you pick me out from all the other girls at that party?' Wondering why me there were so many others, younger with no baggage as Tommy is, not that I would change that for the world.

'I think it was your shoes.'

'My shoes, what shoes, I can't remember which pair I was wearing.' What a funny answer, he liked my shoes.

'I can't remember what pair but it was the state of them.'

'I beg your pardon?'

'The heels were covered in mud and bits of grass stuck to them, I remember it well, made me laugh, there was you dressed to kill with your shoes in an awful state.'

'Oh I do remember, I tried to clean them but had no success by the sound of it.' I started to blush in the dark, hoping he wasn't going to ask me how they got in that state.

'The chap's sister was complaining about the dog and his feet were a dam sight cleaner than yours. You made me smile, I kept watching your boredom, I could see you wanted to leave, so did I.'

I had to remind him he was swimming tomorrow and Tommy would not wait.

He stood over me then bent down and kissed me gently.

'We are going now.' I came too with a jolt, not registering who he was or where I was and going now meant nothing for a second, then remembering everything. I put my arms around his neck and told him to enjoy himself and thankfully went back to sleep.

When I eventually arose, I washed and dressed, trying to look pretty. I started to prepare lunch.

Two o'clock Tommy rushed in still wet-ish and glowing.

'Peter aint half a good swimmer Mum.'

'Say it properly Tom, aint half is not right. Oh forget it.' Peter was a little less excited.

'Not worn out are we?'

'No way.' He collapsed on Jonathan's sofa. I hope he doesn't turn up today.

'Would you like a beer?' I asked Peter, yes, he would as he eyed the glass of coke Tommy had helped himself too.

'Something smells nice.' Peter said referring to my cooking as I handed him a cold beer.

'Our lunch, can you stay, maybe it will be another half hour.'

'You can have me as long as you like.' He waved a hand in my direction but I could see his eyes looking sleepy and red from the chlorine in the swimming pool.

He proceeded to have a nap. If Jonathan

called, they could curl up together.

Tommy was not at all tired, I dragged him from the room to leave Peter in peace.

We sat around the table eating the roast dinner I had cooked, I felt uncomfortable! It was nice, of course it was nice, like a proper family, but I did not like it. Hard to say why it just is not us.

Peter stayed another night in my bed telling me he would be gone by six o'clock as he had to drive to Windsor and the traffic was horrendous. I didn't see him again for three weeks, Tommy thought it was three years and enquired every day was Peter back yet.

Why did I feel so uncomfortable, I did not like Tommy getting this close?

Relationships like this are not meant to last and Tommy would not understand and would be upset. Put a stop to it now was my first response. I found it hard to do so, I liked getting his little text every night, getting longer now. The next time he came our way we had a similar weekend, Peter and Tommy thoroughly enjoying each other's company, I felt a little left out.

Explaining this to Sarah, she understood. She had no true reason for my feelings but assured me she would feel the same.

'Been on our own for too long that is the trouble. Independent, cocky, everything our own way, no one interfering, old women.'

'Yes, old miserable women' I said.

'No way I'm not miserable, well not often,' following that comment with 'seen anything of Jonathan.' He made her miserable, best that she did not see him. It was unavoidable the way he kept calling into the bolt-hole lately, I wonder what Peter would make of that?

Mo Lily

Chapter Ten

Before long I was treated to another Jonathan visit, I was getting fed up with this and his glum face.

'No car?' I enquired.

'No she's took it.' She is Mrs Jonathan after all and well entitled to take the car I guess. He slouched on his sofa again, I made him a coffee, not comfortable he would go soon.

Who would believe it, Sarah had her radar working well today. Within ten minutes, she was at the door.

'Jonathan is in the front room.' I told her as she prepared to settle in the kitchen. Putting a smile on her face, she left me.

I could hear laughter and chat, I could not be bothered with them. Must be an hour later I told them I had to pick up Tuck, my sister's boy from school and my son.

'Okay love.' Said Sarah with no intentions of

leaving, 'Mrs Dawes is picking up my two they are going to a birthday party at Knockdowns.' A place where kids went mad usually knocking each other down.

Still disgruntled with both of them I left to do my chauffer duties, along with a bit of shopping.

When we arrived back home Tommy could hear a noise upstairs and rushed up there to see who it was. I was suspicious, and ventured up my stairs slowly, not wishing this to be true.

Sarah was in the bathroom, Jonathan was in my bed!

'Uncle Jonathan.' Tommy called as he was pleased to see him there and jumped all over him. I stood in the doorway my hands on my hips, shaking my head with the best cross face I could muster.

Slamming and banging, chipping my cups I stayed in the kitchen washing up.

'We are just going love.' Jonathan called to me, Sarah said nothing.

'Good.' I answered and did not turn round from the sink to look at either of them or said goodbye.

They both telephoned me several times that evening seeking my sympathy and approval.

'My bed!' I yelled at Sarah.

'Sorry.'

'Keep me out of it.'

'He can't come here, the kids.'

'I don't care!' And I hung up. A similar phone call from Jonathan, of course he could go to her place but it is the kids.

'Are you frightened of them?'

'Too true I am, have you seen them?'

'You know dam well I have seen them, I don't want to know your problems.' I hung up on him too. There was no sorry, a mistake, it will not happen again, type of conversation.

Jonathan phoned again, late, whispering, because she was about, he was phoning me in secret as all his life was, a secret.

'I can't lose my bolt-hole, I will go mad.'

'It is not your bolt-hole you are having thoughts about it is another hole and I am not getting involved with it, goodnight.'

When I got in bed, after changing the sheets, I was not cross anymore I could see the funny side of it. Thank God, I never had trouble with my Tommy like that, there was never a problem with any Tom, Dick or Harry I brought home. Oh that makes me sound terrible, can I retract that, forget I said it.

I left those two to sort it out themselves and never mentioned it to Sarah she seemed happy and excited all the time and was nice to her rotten kids, I did not see Jonathan for a while.

However, that was not the end of it.

I opened my door one day to find Diane, Jonathan's wife, standing there. Here we go!

'Hello Di won't you come in?'

'No, I won't thanks, I have come to give you a piece of my mind and to tell you to leave my husband alone, he is nothing to do with you.'

'Whoa, whoa, hold on here don't you go pointing your finger at me. In addition, as you well know I have known Jonathan far longer than you have, he always has, and always will be my best friend, nothing else. I would like you to share that same friendship but you don't want to, do you?' She shook her head violently and made that clear.

'My son thinks the world of his uncle and

you will never stop it no matter how much you shake your head. I admit he comes here for a little comfort when he is down in the dumps, that is all.'

'You give him too much comfort,' waggling her finger under my nose 'I know your type and your idea of comfort, you need a license for your knocking shop.'

'Ere, ere watch your mouth Diane. If you paid more attention to your husband he would not need anyone else.'

'So there is someone else, if it's not you, who is it?' Christ what have I said? I can't talk to this woman she must go.

'Nobody, how do I know, please go Di you are making things unpleasant and saying things that you will wish you hadn't.' I was pulling the door too as I spoke, she pushed it open again, kicking it with her foot.

'Watch my door or you will be getting a bill for new paintwork.' She kicked it again, be dammed, then turned round and left.

Whew and I am the innocent party in all this. I phoned Jonathan and filled him in, I said I would phone Sarah and let her know. No need he told me, he was there now and would tell her himself. Give me strength!

My next visitor was Peter full of the joys of spring, pleased to see his little mate, high five and all that and a present.

'Fank's Pete.' Pete indeed, right little mates. Tommy ran upstairs with his present and I got a squeeze and a cuddle.

'Hello darling, I missed you, did you miss me?' I liked it but just nodded in answer to his question.

That night in bed after, well you know, I decided to tell him about Jonathan and Sarah just in case he should be here when a storm blew up.

He loved the story, must meet this chap was his answer to the mess.

'No way, should he turn up you make yourself scarce, he does not know about you, Sarah does that is all. But she would not have told him, she is too wrapped up with their own problems.'

'I am a problem?'

'No you read me wrong. Just be casual and leave, okay.'

'Huh, fine.'

It happened of course, first Sarah arrived

with her kids until she see Peter her intentions were to ask me to babysit, she fortunately changed her mind, though I would not put it past her to ask anyway.

Then Jonathan followed, her unknowing.

'Thanks Jen you're a pal.'

'Hold on here Jonathan.' Sarah was shaking her head at him.

'This is Peter.' I introduced them, remember I told him make yourself scarce. No way, long chats about things that men talk about, lots of yes mate, no mate, same as me old man, ha, ha, ha. I left them to it, Sarah followed me with the very grumpy looking kids.

'Do you want to play in the garden? Or find Tommy he is in his room?'

'No' they just sat there, I pushed a glass of coke each in front of them with straws, just for fun, the little one enjoyed the straw, the big girl threw it on the table.

'They seem to be getting on.'

'Peter gets on with most.'

'And you are saying Jonathan doesn't?' This relationship was touchy. There was always my washing up, as I cluttered with the crocks in the sink.

'Does he go home to Diane at all?' Sarah frowned and nodded to her girls.

'Just get on with it the pair of you, I have had enough of feeling sorry for that cow Diane and don't wish to talk about her.'

I finished wiping my dishes, marched into the front room's laughter, and told Peter we would be late if we did not get a move on.

'Yes, yes sorry love, just having a chat.'

He got up and shook hands with Jonathan.

'We must make some arrangements for an evening out together without the kids.'

'Certainly sounds good to me, we will make a move Jen, see you later.' Jonathan kissed my cheek as Sarah glowered at me from the door.

'Bye Sarah' I said, Peter kissed her cheek. They left, no kids waving just sulky faces in the back. Jonathan what are you at?

'Where are we going?' asked Peter.

'I don't know, just out, they are driving me nuts. You liked him didn't you?'

'Yes he is a nice chap.' We went out with Tommy on to the downs, they kicked the football around, it was my turn to sulk.

I feel I have lost my two best friends to each other and my boyfriend to my son. How sad is that. I might have known from the first in the chemist when he told me to "stay there" that he was bossy.

The director of a large company his life is giving out orders and his staff obey him. Then there is me, what am I? What was Sarah's description of single mums, confident, independent, like our own way and not being told what to do. Attracted to all men, but don't know how to keep one. There is no hope for any of us.

Looking at Peter playing football dreadfully and he was not playing it down for Tommy's sake he really was useless. What am I doing with this bloke?

What is Sarah doing with Jonathan?

Life is a shit.

They came over to me, at last remembering I was there.

'Fancy some lunch?'

'If you like' I answered in a miserable voice that he took up on.

'Oh dear are we neglecting you?' ruffling my hair. I hate that, grandads do that to children when they don't know how to talk to them, it is a, never mind, touch.

'Come on love cheer up.' He gave me a squeeze and a hug. Tommy likes to see other people cuddle his mum, he enjoys the comfort of others feeling like he does, he will never be the jealous type. I tried a smiling face, and took hold of my son's hand as we walked back to the car.

We had lunch in a nice pub that had a kid's garden and a kids menu. It was chosen especially for his new friend. I should be pleased of this, Peter caring about my son not leaving him out, but it made me uncomfortable again. I watched him as he ordered at the bar with Tommy close on his heels not bothered if I was there or not.

Peter would make a good dad he needed a family. He said he was thirty-nine, he should be working on that before he gets too old, finding some younger woman to have his babies, not playing with mine.

He gives me the impression this is a new experience for him. Surely, he has come across children and enjoyed their company before, nieces or nephews, does he have any? I do not know, he never mentions brothers or sisters.

And so the weekend went.

Peter stayed a little longer this time, almost a week, not that I saw much of him, he worked very late most days, just coming back to me to sleep, and that is all he did, just sleep. With much apology, he returned to Windsor, leaving me a bit flat.

Mo Lily

Chapter Eleven

In desperation, I telephoned Les. He knew Sarah and Jonathan as well as I did, we all knew each other from way back, even as far back as school. He is still a friend of Jonathans, though nothing alike. I have to admit he does know me better than he knows Sarah, as she will not have anything to do with his hanky-panky.

He was on a roof at the time of my phone call, he is a scaffolder.

'I'll be round straight after work,' he told me with glee.

'Wash and change first Les.'

'Yeah sure I will. Can you get some yogurt? A large pot you choose your favourite flavour.'

'Aw Les, nothing mucky.'

'Yoghurt's not mucky it clean stuff.'

'I was wondering could we just talk?'

'Talk, come all the way round there to

talk?' I think he nearly fell of his roof with the shock.

'What do you mean, all the way round there, I only live a few turnings from you, you could walk it. Where on earth do you think I live now?'

'Do me tea?' he asked.

'Yes, yes, what time?'

'Six thirty.'

'Okay.' He won't stay all night, no yogurt he will be off before eight to try the yogurt on someone else.

He was early, I was late, while waiting for his tea he played with Tommy, now Les can play football so they argued a bit. Tommy wished Peter was back and told us so over our meal, enlightening Les how they always played nicely together and he did not hog the ball all the time, indicating that Les did.

'Who is Peter then ducks? Got yourself a boyfriend have you? No wonder you didn't get any yogurt.'

Tommy frowned at him.

We had a cup of tea in the front room, Tommy cleared off to play computer games in his room.

'I want to talk to you about Jonathan.'

'Oh no not me, have you seen who he visits regular?'

'Yes they involve me, I don't like it.'

'I had his wife round spitting feathers at me.' He was laughing about it.

'She came here too, kicked my front door.'

'Oo not your best paintwork bet you didn't like that.'

I was out of the norm, I didn't like plastic doors and windows, mine were all the original wood, painted white, professionally, cost me big bucks, but I liked it. Everyone knew about my paintwork, and was under threats not to damage it, Diane knows that as well, that is why she put her foot in.

'He is married you know.'

'Course I know, we went to his wedding Didn't we?'

'Sarah's not.'

'For crying out loud, no she's not.'

'He should have married her, he has always fancied her.' Getting exasperated with him now I began to think this was not such a good idea, requesting we talk.

'I know all this Les.'

'I think he would have married her if it wasn't for her fat kids.' Fed up with him I sighed.

'She would not have had them if he had married her in the first place would she?'

'It wouldn't have lasted, it would be her kicking your paint.'

'Don't you think so?' What did he know beyond a pot of yogurt?   There am I listening to what he has to say.

'Mark my words it will be over soon, let us see how long, shall we have a bet?'

'No we shan't, I am not making bets with you on a subject like that, in fact I would never bet with you at all, you would fix it.'

'Yeah if I could. Thanks for the tea Jen, no yogurt, no "afters" I'd best make a move.'

'Les you are incorrigible, no mistaken marriage for you. A chance would be a fine thing.'

'Get off' he said as he pulled his jacket on 'I'll be the single old man in the rest home looking for some old bid to try my yogurt out on, They will be queuing up for an experience. Say too-da-loo to Tom.' He gave my cheek a peck and my hands a squeeze, telling me, 'don't worry.' He walked home.

Could he possibly be right? I didn't think that way, all I could see was more trouble.

However, he was right, not long after his visit Sarah came to my door, distraught, crying, and hysterical. Her kids refusing to get out of the car, she pushed in my front door.

'He's called it off, called it off the bastard! Gone back to her, why has she taken him back? If he had nowhere to go he would have stayed with me.' I was filling the kettle with water for a cup of tea, which was not going to help much by the look of her.

'Here wash your face under the tap ducks.'

'No, what fucking good would that do?' Yes it was a stupid thing to say I just thought cold water would make her feel fresher but I can see a bucket full over her head wasn't going to make any difference. She moved to the front room and threw herself on Jonathan's sofa.

She did not want her cup of tea either.

'He sleeps here doesn't he?' She said

sobbing into my cushions. Oh Christ I could do without this. Tommy came running in from somewhere.

'What's the matter with her?' he asked.

'She ran over a cat and it has upset her.' The spy quickly answered.

'Fucking cat, he needs running over.' She screamed into the cushions. Tommy's ears pricked up, bad words, he would stay and listen and sat down in an armchair.

Yes I have armchairs as well as this sofa, good job too as the sofa was going to be soaking wet soon.

'Tommy why don't you ask the girls to come in and play in the garden?' I said pointing to Sarah's car.

'Play, they can't play anything,' pointing towards Sarah's little girl.

'She spits!' he said.

'Ohhh no' moaned Sarah.

I am going to get rid of that sofa, hard, wooden chairs that is what I will have, nothing comfortable, this went through my thoughts as I left her curled up in a foetus positing quietly sobbing.

I went out to the girls asked them if they wanted anything, a drink perhaps, at least come indoors.

'Don't want too, when is she coming out?'

'Not for a bit love.'

'We will stay here for a bit then.'

'Would you like a book or something?'

'No way' said the eldest girl digging her elbow into her little sister as she was about to say something. I left them there, looking in on Sarah I asked her.

'What about your girls Sare?'

'To hell with them.' I closed the door.

Two hours later, her girls were asleep in the mucky car. A cup of tea and two paracetamol did not help their mother.

'You cannot carry on like this Sarah I am worried about your children.'

'Don't bother about them they are just showing their disapproval trying to make me worry, no chance.'

She drank her tea very quickly and said she had better go. I was relieved as her car drove off my drive. Les was right it would never work between them two. I wondered how long would it work between Jonathan and Diane come to that.

That evening I had another visit, this time it was Jackie and Bart unusual to see them at my place but this was special, they had come to tell me they were getting married.

Good news, I like Bart he was just right for Jackie they looked so happy, glowing.

Jackie had put on a little weight since her mother died, had her hair cut short and lightened, it suited her, and she was not a nervous wreck anymore.

They were on the way to tell Sarah their news, not a good time right now, I put them off without going into too many details.

Jonathan did go back to his wife, she forgave him, he forgave her, why she needed forgiving I have no idea. Isn't it strange when men are fed up with their wives they seek another woman's company, when wives are fed up with their husbands it puts them off men entirely.

Chapter Twelve

We all, and I mean all, kids as well went to Jackie and Bart's wedding. I thought she would have a small discreet turn out considering how old they both are, both married before, but no, she had the works.

Her son gave her away, his father her first husband is dead, he died after a long illness when his son was fourteen. Jackie did a good job with her mother's help bringing his son up, growing into a fine chap, he is married and lives away from here, she does not see him very often.

Then poor Jackie took on the responsibility of her mother. Not much of a life for her, now this is her time. Mason Bartholomew, Bart, I know nothing about, divorced with three kids that he never sees, his first wife married again ages ago, that is all I know. He has made Jackie happy and that is what matters to me as her friend.

I didn't take Peter to the wedding, I took Tommy.

Mason James Bartholomew, you are on a winner with a name like that, turn it round it is James Mason bet his mum was a fan.

Jackie would now be Mrs Jackie Bartholomew but to us they were just Jack and Bart, could be two guys.

They made us welcome at their wedding, sounds daft but they did, pleased to see us all under one roof. Bart had his mates there, many plumbers I guess.

It was there I met Martin, crikey the other half of Peter. Sorry to tell you he is nice, understated, very nice, and I am not sorry.

Tommy found him, well found his little daughter actually. A sweet four year old who Tommy decided needed his help and guidance, he took her hand, which she gave with pleasure and walked her around amongst the guest. Introduced her to my Uncle Jonathan and Steven, his son, yes even Jonathan's son was there with his father and Diane. This is a friend of my mums and another friend of my mums as he found Sarah, giving the little girl instructions about keeping away from the fat girls.

They eventually got around to me.

'This is my mum. You can call her Jenny, this is Mandy.'

'Hello Mandy.'

'Hello Jenny.'

'We are just going upstairs.'

'Is there an upstairs?'

'Yes and a pool table.' Running now, they rushed off upstairs.

He looked nice, dark hair, dark skin but blue eyes only a little taller than me.

'You met my delightful scrap of joy.' He said, as he slowly looked me up and down.

'Sorry?'

'That is my daughter.'

'Oh I understand, she is quite delightful, my son has taken her over being very protective. I have never seen him take to such a youngster before.'

'She is enjoying it, she has no older

115

siblings, a big boy just talking to her is rare.' We introduced ourselves and spent the rest of the wedding in each other's company.

I was concerned how Sarah would feel here today, as we knew Jonathan would be here with Diane, but I am sorry to say I forgot all about her.

Martin is one of Bart's oldest friends, they do not work together, but their work involves each other, he was telling me, Martin was also in the building trade, turning his hand to most jobs.

'Not as good a plumber as Bart but I give it a go. We went to school together, Bart and Mart, sounds like a shop, we fitted together well, the only trouble they could not remember which was which.'

Our conversation went along similar lines all evening. He was more my type, my class, that sounds uppity but you know what I mean. What was I doing with this Peter? I did not realise but I watched myself when I was with him, like I watched what I said, tried not to swear, a bit of a job with me as I do it without noticing.

I didn't know this Martin so I acted naturally, so did he, it was nice.

Tommy and Mandy came back, she needed the toilet, quick.

'Oh dear, always a problem, I can't take her in the gents again, I had to clear everyone out last time before I took her in as she danced up and down outside telling me to hurry up.'

'Come here I will take her.' Holding another hand eagerly, she came with me quickly. I left Tommy and Martin having a male chat, which certainly turned out to be male bonding as when we got back they were nowhere to be seen. After ten minutes, they came back.

'Come upstairs Mum, you can play pool.' Well I can but we are at a wedding.

'Now?'

'Yes come on Jen' said Martin. I went upstairs with them nobody held my hand but I did feel I was being lead.

We played pool, my son helped me, and Mandy stood on a stool that we found, while her father helped her.

'I am afraid I can't stay until the end I do

have to get Mandy back to bed, she lives with her grandmother who insists on her bed times, I have restricted visiting rights. This is special being a wedding I have her all weekend but must not take liberties or upset her routine.'

'No I understand, she is young and will need her bed before long look at her.' As Mandy yawned Martin quickly picked her up, she rested her head on his shoulder.

'It was nice meeting you both.' I held my hand out to Martin and gave his daughter a little kiss. Saying goodbye to Tommy, Martin turned away, and then turned back.

'Er Jenny I was wondering are you doing anything tomorrow?' Oh God no, I would make sure I wasn't, I smiled and casually managed.

'I don't think so, not much anyway.' He dug in his pocket, shoved a piece of paper and pen at me, no card this time, put your phone number and address on there, I will ring you in the morning.'

Wow, I did, and my name in case he forgot who I was.

'Bye then.' Suddenly feeling shy as I gave

him all my info.

'Where the devil have you been?' shouted Sarah at me 'I looked all over for you.'

'I am sorry Sare we were playing pool upstairs.'

'They have gone, you missed saying goodbye and good luck to them.'

'Did we? Aw what a shame.'

'May as well go ourselves now.' Sarah grumpily said, we left in my car, of course, with Sarah hardly saying a word, upset at seeing Jonathan and Diane I guess.

In the morning, not too early but early enough Martin telephoned, as he said he would, no hello or good morning.

'Hi coming out?' Don't muck about mate straight in.

'Yes okay, where?'

'Anywhere, I'll call for you both in half an hour all right.'

'Whoa, hold on give a girl a chance to get ready.' Quickly thinking what am I to wear sounds like a hurry up job, need to wash my hair, I always give it a wash in the shower. Jeans? Oh, I don't know.

'Come as you are you'll do.'

'I am sure I will, I'm not dressed.'

'Okay I'll make it longer than half hour.'

Blimey "Tommy" I called, I'd better rush.

'We are going out with Martin and Mandy.'

'Are we, how did you manage that?' Cheeky sod 'get ready, hurry up.'

'They are here.' Call Tommy as he rushed out. Fine, nearly ready I called as I finished with the hair. He even looked nice in the day light, a bit outdoorsy and athletic. A nice car an estate and clean, very clean for a builder I thought. I was just about to leave when the phone rang, I paused at the door. Martin heard it, he called from his car where he was still sitting.

'Go on get that we will wait.' I returned to answer the phone expecting Sarah in her usual state, I was wrong it was Peter.

'Good morning sweetness, I am coming your way, see you about lunch time.'

'Oh Peter hello, 'erm oh, I was just going out.' Boy was I panicking, flustered, spluttering, guilty, for Christ's sake what am

I guilty about.

'Going out? A bit early for you, when will you be back?' He was digging now.

'Hard to say I maybe all day.' I didn't know did I? Then, thinking about it I would not want to see Peter later anyway, very difficult. Tommy may say something.

'Yes I think I am most likely going to be all day, we are taking the kids out, can't rush them can you.'

'Okay Jen, not to worry we will give it a miss until tomorrow, see you after work, you girls have a good time. Bye love.'

'Bye Peter.' You girls, I felt awful for almost a minute, then jumped into the car with Martin and our children, we went out for the day, it was all day and I gave Peter Martin no thought at all.

What a day we had, little Mandy is a dream, and her dad aint bad either.

I will not bore you describing the kiddie places where we went. Martin hit it off with Tommy immediately, one thing alone did it. He called him Thomas.

'I'm not calling him that baby name Tommy, he is a big boy.' My baby, I had to also call him Thomas, Mandy being the only one to get away with saying Tommy, he did not mind her using that name as she was only a baby but not me anymore Martin was right he is a big boy.

'Mum, Thomas please or I'll not answer.' I was ordered to comply, all day I kept forgetting, Tommy, 'er Tom, it's "Thomas!" It took a while for me to adjust.

During our day out, I got to know everything and more than I needed to know about Martin. Almost everything I told him about me. It was our life stories, tumbling out of us to strangers, however as I now know so much about him I cannot call him a stranger can I?

When we said goodnight that was all we said, our two babies, well my big boy, was knackered, sorry worn out, tired. Martin agreed they were knackered, Peter would have said shattered. Oh well.

That night when Peter sent my text adding something about missed you today, I chucked the phone on the bed talking to myself I said "Clear off."

Now that is not nice is it? He is a nice

chap, I like him, yes, I still do but there has always been a big But between us.

My sister babysat for a couple of hours the next day as Peter wanted to spend some time alone with me and he wanted us to have a nice relaxing meal, something to do with missing me extremely.

Not the same here mate, I did not tell him.

He was a bit peeved I did not ask him to Jackie's wedding and wanted to know about it. I didn't ask him because he did not know Jackie very well and at first, I thought it was to be a quiet affair.

Peter was here all week, Martin did phone again, I had to tell him I was busy at work, a lie, and could not manage this week.

'Fair enough, take my phone number and give me a ring when the emergency is over.' I wrote it down and squirrelled it away for a time when Peter had returned to Windsor.

He didn't go quickly enough for me, oh dear what am I like.

Mo Lily

Chapter Thirteen

When free, I telephoned Martin he was surprised to hear from me.

'I thought you gave me the brush off.' See no diddling about, straight in.

'I am sorry was I rude?'

'No just me not believing you.' Oops, he felt my lies.

'Can you get away tonight?' he asked.

'Well Tommy, you know in the middle of the week as well.' I did erm and um a bit 'why don't you come round here, we can babysit together?'

'Babysit that big boy.' He laughed. I forgot Thomas not Tommy.

'Afraid so' I told him.

'I don't mind, do you like telly?'

Oh, heck he was one of those blokes who cannot be in a room without the television being on all the time.

'Well some things.' I slowly said.

'That's good because I can't stand much on there either and I don't relish a whole evening watching whatever they throw at you.' What a relief, a man not interested in watching a screen notwithstanding what is beyond.

'I thought all men liked watching telly?'

'Did you?' He said no more.

'About seven or eight-ish how about that?' I said

'Seven-ish definitely, bye.'

I was still at work it was lunchtime again. I had better get a move on when I get home I expect the place is like a tip, I will have to shift myself, seven he said, tidy up, have tea, homework, make myself beautiful, I wished.

Tommy, Thomas was full of himself when we got home.

'I may have a mate coming round later so I want this mess cleared up.' Pointing mainly his rubbish strewn around the lounge, the dining room and the hall, not at this stage telling him who was coming.

Dropping his school stuff anywhere, he

added to the mess.

'Aw I have homework to do.' Preferring to do homework rather than tidy up, most unusual. We had a quick tea, very quick.

I surveyed the front room, clean and nice.

'Tommy get ready for bed.'

'My homework.' he moaned, I would forgot about that.

'Who's coming anyway, the Queen?' he cheekily asked tutting at me.

'It is Martin actually and we want to make a good impression don't we?'

'Martin, Mandy's dad, how did you manage that?'

'Don't you be so cheeky, managed it easily in fact.' He was giggling at me.

'Do you like him Mum?'

'Why do you ask?'

'Because I do, that's all.'

They greeted each other noisily as Tommy rushed to let him in.

'This is our house.' Thomas was telling him, of course, it is our house, we briefly said "Hi" as Thomas excitedly told him to come upstairs and see his room.

Thomas has a nice room, overlooking the

back garden, as you know, they both hung out the window viewing the surroundings, he whispered to Martin.

'Don't worry I am going to bed soon and you two can be alone. I will show you my stuff first. There is this and this.' as he got his treasures out from special places giving them to Martin to look at.

I stood by the doorway watching my son, he did so like a man's company, always with me and Sarah and her girls, we never had many boys come round, he loved it when Steven, Jonathan's son came but that was only once a month. I left them to it, telling Tommy bed in ten minutes.

Martin came downstairs.

'He is in bed reading a book on history, part of today's homework.'

'That's fine.'

'You have a nice house here Jen, looks in good repair.' He said banging the walls.

'Here watch it I want it to stay that way.' Forgetting he is a builder.

'Can I look outside before it gets dark?'

'Well if you want too.' We went outside I

showed him my garden but he was looking up at the gutters, and my wooden windows.

'You haven't any plastic windows, even a wooden front door I noticed.'

'Yes that is me while they last I will keep them, I do not like plastic much and they do not last forever not as long as these lovely wooden frames.' We went on to talk about the drain position and bricks and pointing and snots, that are the cement runs between the bricks, I haven't got any apparently.

He looked at my house as some men look at a woman's body.

'It is getting chilly Martin can we go in?'

'Sorry, yes, I will look at the front another day.' Will you mate, I haven't asked for a survey, whatever you say will not put me off our house.

We sat on the settee drinking the wine he brought along with him.

'How's your loft?' he asked. Give over!
'It's fine.'

'Do you go up there often?' I told him no.

'How do you know all is well up there?'

'Nothing untoward has happened so I presume everything is fine and leave well alone.'

'I will take a look for you.'

'Not now you won't.'

'No not now, another day.' Oh dear so this is what builders were like. We got over the house chat and proceeded on to chat that is more comical. Talking and laughing about nothing much we were very relaxed in each other's company.

Suddenly he put his arm along the back of the sofa the other arm across me and lent on the sofa arm my side.

'Can we get familiar?'

'What sort of question is that?' A bit surprised at such a strange approach.

'That's me being polite.'

'Oh very polite.'

'Well you are a mum, not a twenty year old up for grabs.'

'So that is your polite approach to the old mums?'

'Not all, just some.' He was taking the piss, laughing at me. I took his face in both my hands and proceeded to snog him. He let me carry on still leaning over, responding but not touching me.

Then he pulled me onto my feet and took

charge. Coming up for air, I told him.

'Martin the curtains are open.'

'So they are.'

'The light is on.'

'So it is.'

'And you are kissing my left breast for all to see.'

'So I am, very nice it is too.' I took his hand leading him upstairs I told him,

'Turn the light off.'

We made quick passionate, almost desperate love. I guess he does not do it often. Not like me getting laid in all directions. The second time was slower, nice romantic, one could say.

The bedroom door burst open.

'Are you two staying there all day? I have to go to school!' There was Tommy fully dressed in his school uniform.

'Christ is that the time?' Martin jumped out of bed stark naked. Tommy looked him up and down.

'You've got a big willy.' He said as I pulled the covers over my head.

'Go back to sleep love I will take Thomas to school.' They left me in peace. I didn't sleep, I thought about work, did I get any sleep at all last night? I can't go to work today, not just yet they owe me time, I will go this afternoon.

I had a phone call about eleven o'clock, a sheepish voice speaking to me.

'Hello just wondered if you went to work?' It was Martin.

'No but I will go this afternoon, how are you managing to work with no sleep?'

'Not very well, I am packing it in at lunchtime, see you before you go.'

'Will you, okay.' Martin came for an hour before I left. He ate the sandwiches I had prepared for him with relish, I just had a coffee after my late breakfast. I put the posy of flowers he gave me into a small bowl that was sweet of him, being polite to an old mum again.

'I have to go.' I told him.

'I will crash out in your bed.' He told me.

'Please yourself.'

When I got home, he had gone, gone where? I do not know where he lives, not far

I guessed.

Tommy came home from school had his snack in the kitchen that he liked to have before tea always hungry after school.

'Was Martin here all night?' Oops now what?

'Yes.' I said no more.

'That's okay.' Got his permission by the sound of it, neither of us said anything else. I felt a bit like a teenager answering me dad.

Martin called in that evening but did not stay all night, some problem he had to attend to at work.

I did not see him but received plenty of phone calls for the rest of the week.

Mo Lily

Chapter Fourteen

Peter arrived unannounced I was completely taken by surprise, it could have been last week when Martin was here.

'Jenny, Jenny a holiday for us. A holiday in the South of France! I have just flown back, it is wonderful, you will love it. Oh dear, come here.' He threw himself on Jonathan's sofa and pulled me on his lap.

'A friend of mine, a very dear friend, is retiring from his business, he has offered me first refusal to a very liquid company and everything to do with it which includes his home, not far from the head office. A villa, what a villa, you are going to love it.

I will take you there next week, a small quiet place not far from Monte Carlo, you have been there?'

'No.' I said, he did not pause or listen.

'We will go for a month, just a few things to arrange in Windsor.' He gave me a tight excited squeeze.

'Hold on, hold on here. I am a mum, Tommy has to go to school, I have to go to work, and we can't just go off to the South of France for a month.' I pulled myself up from his lap.

'Jenny you won't have to work in that little solicitor's office again.'

'That is what you think of it some little solicitors office, to me it is just as important as your job is to you.' I was getting huffy.

'Jenny darling,' he reached out for my hand 'I want you to marry me, come and live in France as my wife.' I stared at him in shock 'I mean it, say yes' he said to my shocked look.

'No!'

'Come on Jen don't be silly you don't need time to think about it.'

'What about Tommy?'

'He comes with us.'

'But school in France, he won't like that, he won't understand anybody.'

'Then he can go to boarding school in England' I was horror-struck that he could say such a thing.

'What? Boarding school! You must be

joking, my son in a boarding school in another country, I wouldn't send him to a boarding school if it was just up the road.' Getting huffy now was nowhere near the right word to use I was a dam sight more than huffy.

'I always went to a boarding school it was great fun'

'I expect that was because your home life was naff.'

'Jenny stop please, you are giving it no consideration just think about us and a life in France. I could not get home quick enough to tell you, anyone else would jump at a chance like this.'

He we go Jen…

'You'd better find "anyone else" because none of this includes me and Tommy, we like it here and here is where we intend to stay, enjoy your life in the villa with anyone else, whoever it is, we are not interested.

Will you leave now Peter?' The utter astonishment on his face had he ever been told to leave before? Nobody talks to him like that, he is the boss who manages their lives tells them what to do and when to leave.

"Stay there!" remember.

Slowly he got up still reaching for my hand giving me a sympathetic look.

'I'll phone you tonight.'

'You won't have time to actually make a phone call, text only is all you can manage.' Why did I say that I don't care a fiddler's fuck if he phones or sends a stupid goodnight text.

Thank God, Tommy was not home, he was next door with Samantha. Imagine me telling him he was leaving England and leaving Sam, they would run away together.

It did seem I was making Tommy my excuse but the truth was I did not want to go to France or anywhere with Peter Martin.

I did get a text a lot longer than usual,

'Did I feel any better?' Indeed, I ignored it as usual. The next day came a phone call from Windsor, and another goodnight text. I'm getting pissed off with him now.

Saturday morning I had a phone call.

'Hi Hun.' it was Martin. Thank goodness someone normal.

'Hello Martin, how you doing?' I

cheerfully said.

'You sound pleased to hear me.'

'Yes I think I am.' Dam well please it's not Mr Martin.

'I am free for the weekend, I want to see you both.'

'Okay fine.' I was trying to think what I can say to Peter should he turn up unannounced again like last time.

'And guess who is coming again, Mandy.'

'Lovely Tommy will be pleased. Where shall we take her?'

'I was wondering would you like to come here?'

'What to your home, lovely.' Perfect if Peter came round we wouldn't be here.

'It is not that wonderful, don't get excited.'

'Sorry when shall we come?'

'All weekend, I've got room.'

'It sounds nice Martin thanks, like going on holiday for the weekend, we are always here it will be nice for us both.'

'Can you get ready in an hour?'

'Certainly can.'

'Pick you up at eleven o'clock bye.' When I told Tommy, he didn't care about leaving

Sam, as he wanted to see Mandy.

'They are here' called Tommy as he ran out climbing into the back of Martin's car.

'Hello.' I could hear his cheerful voice, I followed him equally pleased to see them. Tommy was putting a shoe back on Mandy's foot that had come off, falling to the floor, she was strapped into her baby seat and could not reach.

'Hi ya ducks you look nice.' Blimey, I muttered my thanks to him, I did nice in such a hurry. We set off, heading towards to the duel carriageway.

'Are we going to yours?' I asked

'Yes you said it was okay.'

'You don't live just round the corner as I thought.'

'No did I ever say I did?'

'I just thought, oh forget it.' He did not live out of town but the other side of town, if you know what I mean, we took the duel carriageway to avoid the traffic. I did not know this part of town, it was a bit posher than my side. In fact I did not have a clue where we were or where he lived, I somehow imagined a flat on his own, I couldn't be more wrong.

'This is it.' Casually he said turning the car between high hedges. There was a beautiful Georgian style house, detached from any other.

'This is yours?' I rudely asked in surprise.

'Yes all mine.' He ushered the kids out and Mandy led the way through a side gate and they disappeared into what I presumed was the back garden.

I stood looking at the property, Martin joined me, looking with love at his home.

'To your approval mam?' He said as he looked at it with pride. It dawned on me.

'You built it didn't you?'

'Certainly did, every little bit, outside of the lorry drivers who delivered the materials. I would have no help. Did it myself, I can't tell you the satisfaction it gives a builder to build his own home.'

'I can imagine, Martin you are so clever, how long did it take you?'

'A while I suppose, on and off between other work, I have photos at all stages, you can see them if you are interested. Come and see the inside.' No wonder he poked about in my house when he lives in a place like this, mine must seem awful to him.

We spent at least an hour looking at walls, plumbing, windows, this here, and that there.

Returning to an enormous kitchen, he produced our lunch from the fridge.

'Call the kids in love while I lay the table.' Gosh, this was great it is usually mum's job to lay the table and prepare the food.

All hands washed and seated we started on the enormous lunch. A salad but so much else to it.

'What do you want to do after lunch?' Martin asked.

'Can we stay here?' asked Tommy.

'Okay by me Thomas but we must ask the ladies first it would be rude not to ask them first don't you think?'

'No stay here by all means.' Mandy was nodding with her mouthful.

'Will you come into the garden Mum, there is so much to see, a swing a slide and a Wendy house, all down there he pointed beyond where you could not see. And a horse that lives over the back, he comes for carrots but we didn't have any.'

'I will.' I said looking forward to this.

'And there is a swing bed like Auntie Jackie's got, you two can sit on that and let your dinner go down.'

'Thanks Thomas, you don't mind?'

'No you two won't bother us.' I looked at Martin we grinned at him and each other.

That is what we did, after putting the dishes in the "dishwasher" huh, then feeding the horse with carrots, and opening the bottle of wine that appeared on a little table with two glasses.

We stretched out on the swing bed together, while the children played. It was more than pleasant, bleeding lovely.

'I had no idea Martin.' I said referring to his beautiful house and his life.

'I guess you had no reason to have any idea, about anything, does it matter?'

'You know it doesn't.'

It was a good weekend we all enjoyed it, not venturing off Martin's property we felt there was no need to go out anywhere. Mandy was to be taken back by five o'clock on Sunday, dropping us off first.

Understandably, it would be frowned upon if he turned up at her grandmother's house with us in the car. The usual, will phone you later business and they left.

He didn't phone he called in to see me on his way coming back.

'The Bull has turned into a Pig.' He moaned with a sour face.

'What is all this farmyard talk about?' I tittered.

'It is no laughing matter Jen.'

'Oh serious is it, what has happened who is Bull and pigs as well?'

'She is worse than a cow so I call her the Bull and she is acting like a pig to my Mandy I could tell Mandy's reaction when I drop her off, her sad face.'

'Mandy, she is her granddaughter? Surely not, she would not be unkind to her, why would she do that?' Mystified as no woman treats children badly it is nature for us to nurture them, he must be mistaken.

'She has a son.'

'Good for her, I have a son.'

'No Jen not like that she has an older son

also living with her, Mandy's uncle who comes first in her eyes.

She made some comment about Mandy will have to take a back seat and can't expect to come first all the time.

She grabbed Mandy off me and strode into her house. You should have seen her little face, looking back, after such a lovely weekend I could tell she did not want to be left there.' He sat down looking worried.

'I see what you are getting at, maybe it will be fine who cannot love your Mandy?'

'He rules his mother and now he rules Mandy he is a stuck up domineering prick.'

'Are you just saying that or is he?'

'Okay I am just saying that, they still have my daughter and I don't.'

'It is my little girl I am concerned about, they could move away, go abroad, anything and I would never see Mandy again, Aw.'

'Stop it you have your rights, do you mind if I ask about her mother?'

'She's dead.'

'Oh sorry I didn't mean to snoop.'

'She left when she was pregnant with my baby, and I was so looking forward to it.

She moved back with her mother as she didn't want to be saddled looking after me and a kid.' He drew in a deep breath then let it out slowly. This sounded complicated and a bit hard to grasp, guess you feel the same.

I made a cup of tea.

In the kitchen sitting at the table clutching our cups Martin started to explain from the beginning.

He got Moose pregnant, yeah Moose that is what the man said her name was, don't ask, anyway as explained she returned to her mother shirking any responsibility. Up to this point I thought, poor mum.

She had her baby a daughter all very friendly, Martin was even there at the birth. Her mother has never denied that Martin is the father.

Then Moose recovered from her pregnancy decided to visit America for six months. Poor mum again.

There was an accident, Martin is not sure if it was a car accident or a horse, plane or camel no that is Egypt. She came home on a stretcher! Never to walk again or live long.

Refusing to see Martin meant he did not

get to see Mandy at all. Her brother living with his mum didn't mind and kept out of the proceeding up until this point, he had just hoped she would return, take her baby and go back to Martin keeping out of his and mother's life, especially his.

After the accident her mother nursed her, the brother kept her, Martin had a standing order made by his bank to maintain the baby. She died almost one year later. They never told Martin, he never went to her funeral.

Eventually finding out from a friend he asked to take his daughter, only to be told, no he could not have her or see her. She was all the mother had left of her daughter and would be keeping her baby.

'But you have your rights, is your name on the birth certificate?'

'No just hers, we were never married.'

'Oh you did say ex-wife.'

'I know it is easier.'

Christ this was a muddle, no wonder he was upset, he was lucky he gets to see Mandy at all.

'And the stuck up prick?' There he has me calling him names and I do not even now the man.

'He sees his mum, not a young woman any longer taking on too much. Moreover, his mother's attention turning from him to his sister's baby. A selfish sister who he could not stand and I get the feeling he cannot stand her baby either. He is wrong about his mother's feelings he will always come first. My feelings, my rights do not come into the equations.'

'Martin what a muddle.' I sympathised with him, still only grasping parts.

'I must admit her mother has done a good job with my daughter. All would be fine if it was not for her son and her age of course, she is getting on now, it is a lot for her I do understand.

I have offered to share the responsibility, more than just an odd weekend. I am sure Mandy would be better living with me. But she will have none of it.'

'Mm' was all I could say.

'One thing for sure I will never have a baby again without getting married first.' He made me smother a laugh as he sounded like a fallen woman who would not have sex again until she was wed.

'Oh fuck it, I can't be bothered thinking about it, I get too depressed, sorry love am I swearing too much?'

'No I like a fuck now and again.'

'Hearing one or having one' he asked with a grin.

'Both.'

'You have heard it, how about doing it? Where is Thomas?'

'In bed.'

'I think that is where we should be.' Just the idea cheered him up, in the distance, I heard my mobile phone bleep. I had a goodnight text.

Mo Lily

Chapter Fifteen

It was around a month, six weeks or so later before Mandy came again. During this time, I had an almighty row with Peter. He called to see me, made arrangements first, if you don't mind, an appointment was made fitted in between important stuff.

He came all the way from Windsor specially. You can hear him saying it can't you? When he got here, he did much pacing up and down my lounge saying the well-rehearsed words he had for me, persuasive words. They didn't work, I was on top form and had an answer for every well thought out question.

It turned into pleading. Then the loving bit, came last you notice. He could not manage his life without me now. What a load of drivel. I could see going to France setting up home there, he would need a wife to support him. He would be doing a lot of entertaining, French and English clients, welcoming them to spend some time at his villa.

He brought photos of the place to show me, it was nice, I had to admit. Large place it had its own swimming pool and domestic help to care for everything. Overlooking the sea, he said something about a yacht but I wasn't listening, can't swim can I, don't do boats at all.

He was losing his temper, he grabbed me holding me tight, kissing me into submission. It didn't work.

'Get off me,' I shoved him 'go to fucking France and leave me alone.' I yelled at him. Tommy appeared in the doorway.

'Leave my mum alone.' he shouted at Peter. This seemed to pull him together he looked at Tommy.

'You are right, I will leave your mum alone. Goodbye.' Without another look at me, he left.

'You all right Mum?' asked Tommy as he ran and cuddled me.

'Yes love thanks for your help, he has gone, gone for good. He just would not listen I do not want to go to France.'

'To France? Perhaps a holiday would be nice' he said looking at me seriously.

'It wasn't just for a holiday Tom, it was him he is not our sort is he?'

'Nah.'

We never have our girl's nights anymore.

Jackie's married.

Ruth still looking for her Mr Right decided she was not going to find him on a girl's night, so moved in other circles. The gym, the reading group, Countryside Friends, whatever that is?

So far she had not found a man but made many friends. She is so fussy, you know what she is like, it takes her ages to choose an armchair let alone a man to sit in it.

Her daughter who she has spoilt all her life is turning into, a girl who is grateful, they are very close, very similar in their looks and ways. Ruth being so small looks a lot younger that her age, they are often taken as sisters. They never enlighten the person who makes the mistake.

Sarah got the message from Jonathan and Diane, keeping away but is always looking for a chink in their relationship, never giving up, hoping that one day she will get Jonathan back, perhaps it meant waiting until her daughters had left home.

While waiting they drove her mad, getting so rude, always in trouble at school, every week they came home with a letter or she received a phone call and they needed to see her at the school.

What happened to all this "doing their job" business?

They stole from a shop and were arrested. She had to take them to the police station to be reprimanded, as it was their first offence they got off lightly.

Due to the embarrassment, they never did it again, but apart from that did not care a cuss that they had upset their mother.

Sadie has Malcolm living with her, he is nice, I do not know how she met him. He is too good for her, but adores her and she does him.

'It can't last,' she tells us all 'but I am going to dam well enjoy it while I can.' Every day she is amazed that he comes home to her.

She is pretty, and good at sex so I understand, perhaps that is the attraction. She is into games and dressing up, he must be as well. Takes all sorts.

I am with my Martin, bless him, he really is kind and sweet, my sort of man, he loves Thomas, treats him like his own. We see as much as we can of each other, that really means he is here all the time, we go to his house at the weekend when Thomas has no school. When darling Mandy comes for the weekend, we make it special for her.

In doing so, it is special for us. I never heard from Peter again, not even a glimpse, lunchtime is when I most fear I will bump into him.

I wonder if he did move to France.

Jonathan did not come to see me for a long while. I rather missed the upheaval, I missed seeing him, and so did Tommy.

After a slow ring on the doorbell, I

opened the door to find Jonathan there.

'Not again?' were my first words.

'No love I just came to see you'

'What no row, no sofa, no bolt-hole?'

'No just me I missed you.'

'Well thank God for that, come in.' He looked well, not tearing his hair out that made a change.

'Where is Tommy?' he asked.

'Next door he has a girlfriend.'

'A quick worker, what is she like?'

'Not so quick, it has been a while, almost since they moved in. You have been out of it for so long Johnny, when you have called here you was too depressed to notice.'

'I was, things are better with me and Di now, my fault entirely.'

'Certainly was, she really had a go at me and Les but I like Di just the same.'

'Les? Don't know why Les, but he needs someone to have a go at him. He's got worse if he wasn't my mate I would be disgusted with him, well I am disgusted at times and you entertain him.'

'Don't go down that road Jonathan, that is between me and Les and only believe half what he says, he winds you up.'

'I'm fed up with you, I don't want to think about it.'

'Fed up with me what a cheek.'

'Go and get Tommy I want to talk sense to someone.' I called over the fence for them to tell Tommy his Uncle Jonathan was here, he came running in bringing Samantha with him. Jonathan approved of her he said they were suited.

Before he left, I noticed he gave Tommy some money, a lot by the look on Tommy's face.

'It's not my birthday.'

'No it is a thank you, can you treat your mum for me?'

'Yes I will.' Tommy and Sam looked at the money Jonathan shrugged his shoulders at me.

I smiled and mouthed thank you.

Sadie always had more money than any of us, it was invested for her children's future, she told us. Two kids a boy and a girl, the Lush, Tommy's first love.

She was Lush, not just Tom's idea, most boys thought the same, she liked the attention and succumbed to sex at the young age of fourteen, and yes became pregnant.

She thought she would keep the baby, Sadie thought different.

'Keep a baby when you are fourteen don't be ridiculous. You will get rid of it straight away.' The Lush objected, Sadie dragged her round to see her single mum friends. Us! One after another we had to talk to her explain life as we see it, hoping we could be of help, explain the problems we have encountered and have to deal with alone.

Not until you are confronted with this problem can you see it in true light what it entails, telling a child she has to get rid of a baby is hurtful and unkind to put it mildly, none the less sensible, considering the circumstances. I felt sad when it was my turn to be included in the talks.

Sarah agreed whole-heartedly, confirming she should have got rid of her first child when she had the chance. As they looked out into the garden at her latest escapade, Black Magic, sacrifice and blood dropping, pricking all the kids thumbs and making them rub thumbs with each other, while she mumbled special words over them putting her hands on the top of their heads

'She is unnatural, I caught her with a worm on a stick and matches.' Sarah told Lush who was only two years older 'imagine you get one like that. No bloke will look at you again. Get rid of it.' This had more effect on her than anything her mother or we had said to her about babies. The idea of "no blokes looking at her again" was unthinkable.

Upset and crying, she had an abortion. Sadie's turn to be thankful to the National Health for their facilities, she was put on the pill immediately.

Reconsidering her children's future Sadie decided to spend her money on something she had always wanted. A teashop, sort of, not just teas, everything, she was a very good cook with a total joy for cooking, therefore her teashop was a success.

It was in a busy shopping area she served

the shoppers with elevenses, lunch and afternoon tea, never in the evening she closed when the other shops closed.

Homely and clean, excellent food, she is as busy as hell. Warm and cosy in the winter, tables outside in the summer. We all pay her a visit when shopping, sometimes we arrange a time so we all get there together and Sadie takes time out to join us for lunch.

Martin and I see a lot of Jackie and Bart because the two men are the best of friends.

I found out more about Martin from Jackie, little things that Bart tells her. What a time Martin had had with the "Bull's" daughter. She never wanted Mandy but was frightened to terminate the pregnancy, she seemed to think we would be punished for doing such a thing, maybe she is right.

So she went ahead and had Mandy and almost hating her, and Martin. She gave him no warning she was returning to her mother before the baby was born.

Martin was very upset took him ages to get accustomed to this he did so want a baby. He put all his energy into building his house.

'We all tried to help' said Bart 'but he was not having any of it. He built the house alone. Only in the last couple of years have they allowed him to see his daughter, he missed all her baby years. Now it is only as the grandmother is getting older and her son's persuasion to make her take a rest.

One evening the four of us out together who should I bump into but Les. I went over to have a chat with him, rather than him coming to me, he is such a loose cannon, he could put his foot in it, say anything. This was one person in my past that Martin knew nothing about.

After the usual "Hello's" Les told me how he missed me. I told him I did not miss him.

'No you are all loved up now ducks.'

'Do not be daft I am in my thirties.'

'So?' He took a good look at Martin.

'I know him.'

'Do you really, how come?'

'He is Martin Anderson.'

'Yes that's right, how funny, I don't think he knows you.'

'No I am just a scaffolder, he is the governor of the Anderson Team.'

'Is he, what's that?' I was puzzled what was Les talking about, I had not heard of any team. Les did get strange ideas at times.

'Hasn't he told you what he does?

'Yes he is a builder.'

'Some builder Jen, the "Anderson Team" his name is Anderson.' Les again, his life is full of riddles, why is he involving me in his stories. Though he was right about Jonathan and Sarah, what else did he say?

'Jonathan and Diane how are they, do you know?' Changing the subject on to them away for Martin.

'Oh him, he is frightened to move, can't risk an upset again. He knows it won't last.' He shrugged his shoulders at me.

'Les don't put the mockers on it, they are fine now anyone can see that.'

'He won't be fine until he meets his grannie, Jonathan needs a grannie to be happy.'

He was right again, on Jonathan's fiftieth birthday, he did not go home he went off with Shirley, a grannie twice over. He left Diane, left us all moved to South Wales. I miss him so much, so does Thomas. We do have some super holidays in Wales with him, which is nice but he never comes to see us. He seems to be happier than he has ever been, no need for a bolt-hole. His son Steven joined the army, so none of us sees much of either of them.

When alone with Jackie I asked her about the Anderson Team, did she know what Les was talking about? Yes she did, Bart often did work for them.

'I am not sure how it works. Why don't you ask Martin it is his team, his idea?'

'I can't Jack, he must tell me.' It left me mystified until Bart spoke up for me when we were all together another time.

'Martin explain to Jenny what the Anderson Team is all about, she needs to be told properly as it is confusing for her.'

'You understand don't you Jen?'

'No you haven't told me.'

'I have you don't listen, it is just a group of tradesmen I can rely on, we have become a team. People give me work as a team and

I round up the necessary men to do the work. We are famous I think, Bart what do you say?'

'We certainly are we give a good service and have a good reputation, the orders we take on are getting larger and better, you will be a rich man one day Mart.'

'Sounds like a lot of arranging to me, how do you manage?' I said.

'It is I couldn't do half without my Linda.'

'Linda who is she?' New to me this one.

'Just in the office love.'

This played on my mind "my Linda" I had to find out. Bart told me the address of this office and one day when I knew they were working away, I paid this office a visit just to hang around, looking like I did at Martin Merchants, there I was to meet "my Linda". It was not an office, just a hut in a builder's yard, no blue glass or gold leaf.

On the telephone was a large middle-aged woman, a pencil behind one ear and the telephone to the other, she waved a hand at me to take a seat. I was not going to be able to make the hasty retreat I intended, I would make up something. I sat down listening to her telling someone Mr Anderson was not there but she would tell him, Mr Anderson this and Mr Anderson that all the way through her conversation.

Every time she mentioned Martin's name I raised my eyebrows. She mouthed sorry to me and tried to get rid of the person on the other end of the telephone. Hanging up the receiver, she turned to me.

'How can I help you love?' Not in a snooty way like the woman had asked at Peter's office.

'Nothing really I was just passing and wanted to meet you. You are Linda?'

'Yes I am.' Looking at me puzzled at first then her face relaxed.

'You must be Jenny.'

'You know me?'

'I feel I do love I hear so much about you and your Thomas from Mr Anderson.'

'Really he is daft, what does he say?'

'Only nice things dear, don't fret.' She got up from her chair with a struggle, as she was well overweight, opening the office door to the yard, some office she called out.

'Bill, tell that Hazel to get back in here and answer the phone like she is paid to do. Now!' He had a Hazel as well, Mm.

'This isn't much to you is it love? But this is what a builder's office is like, it is a very relaxed atmosphere, friendly most times.' Hazel burst in the door.

'Where you been Hazel, off with that new bloke again haven't you?'

'No.' a straight from school, girl said, thumping into a chair at what must be her desk 'the phones not ringing.' she stated as she looked at it.

'But it has been and we have a visitor, you stay here and answer it, don't go away, come Jenny.' She marched me to the other end of the prefabricated office and through a door into a cheerful, tidy office.

'This is Mr Anderson's office he would never forgive me for letting you stay in the cabin. Do sit down.' I felt awkward I should not have come, Martin is not going to like this.

'I was wondering Linda if I should go as Martin is not here?' I didn't sit down.

'Up to you love, I don't think he will be

back today.'

'Linda can I ask you a favour, would you keep my visit from Martin 'er Mr Anderson. I was being a bit nosey.'

'I see that's okay with me you haven't been here, we haven't met.'

'Thanks Linda I'd best go.'

'He is very fond of you, you do know?'

'Well yes I suppose.'

'Be kind to him love he deserves to find happiness.'

'I will try Linda.' What a strange thing for a secretary to say, I presume she is his secretary he just said he could not manage without her, so she could be anyone.

By the way she spoke she much-admired Martin and in just that short time, I could tell she must be a great asset to him. Not just a secretary, maybe a relation, a sister, no nothing like him. What did it matter I felt bad about going there now, how nosey, I wish I hadn't gone, I won't tell anyone.

Why should I care who Linda is, I am jealous, no I am not, not now I have seen her but I was, why? I am never jealous. Martin is just a friend like all my other blokes, I am not looking for Mr Right, just a nice friend who I feel comfortable enough to go to bed with, and is accepted by Tommy.

Moreover, to be able to say goodbye easily when the time comes and still be friends.

Is this Martin any different to the others? I do like him, but I liked Peter until he got on my nerves.

Martin is a sad case when it comes to his daughter, perhaps I feel sorry for him, no, I feel sorry for his little girl. She is so sweet such a lovely nature and pretty, cute, a good child all those things that you cannot resist in a youngster, and there she is living with people who don't really want her.

Children can notice these vibes, it will spoil her. Poor little mite, living with these old people she never talks of friends, I can just imagine how she is left out, not ill treated, but ignored.

When she is with us she is the centre of attention, Tommy makes sure of that. Then the poor thing has to go back to a man who is not her father and an old lady. Mandy favours her father in looks, so I guess is nothing like her mother yet her grandmother is looking for her daughter's replacement.

I am getting involved here with my own feelings, I can't change things so I should not dwell on it. It is a shame for Martin, perhaps in time she will let him have Mandy more often.

Where do I come in all this, just sitting on the side enjoying their company for the time being.

Why the hell am I worried about "my Linda", oh I should not have gone there. Shall I tell him? How shall I react if he finds out? When he finds out, he is bound to hear something, I must tell him. Oh!

They worked away all week, Bart also. Jackie came to see me, I told her where I had been.

'You like Martin don't you?'

'Yes he is very nice, you know he is.'

'I mean really like him.' She grinned at me over her coffee cup. I unusually flustered over a bloke, moved a few things around on the table trying to find words, the more she grinned the more I blushed.

'Hey, Jenny's in love.'

'Get off, am not.'

'Would you know love if it came to you, not that experienced with it are you?' She looked at me seriously, not joking.

'What do you mean by that? Not experienced, that's a joke'

'Oh you are experienced all right but not where love is concerned, have you ever been in love?'

'I love Tommy.'

'Not that sort of love, the love that hurts when it ends, hurts so much you feel you can't go on without that person.' She gazed into space obviously, she knew what she was talking about.

'You sound like a novel Jack, it's not like that in real life.'

'Isn't it? Don't you believe it, maybe not to you yet.' I changed the subject it was getting too personal because I could not talk about Martin it made Jackie surer she was right and me surer she was not going to be right.

In love, falling in love? To hoot with it, not for me.

After she had gone I went upstairs looked

at myself in my dressing table mirror, I leant on the table and leaned forward staring into the mirror trying to see my soul.

To hell with it I would go out tonight, see who is around, make a new friend, I never have trouble doing that.

I went to see Sarah.

'Go out you must be joking, look at me, I have not been to the hairdressers for weeks, nothing to wear, no baby sitter, besides going out is the last thing I'd want to do, I would be a misery, I'd get drunk and you would be pissed off with me. No way, you all go without me.'

'That's just it Sarah, it is only me and you now, Jackie no way, Sadie is worn out after closing the shop and Ruth goes out with her daughter to the eighteen year old places, I am not setting foot in any of them, they make me look ninety. Please Sarah.'

'No, what about this Martin gone off him have you?'

'No he's still there.'

'Shitting on him then?'

'No don't say it like that, he is nice I wouldn't do that.' I took umbrage to what she was saying.

'Why do you want to go out on the prowl, be satisfied with what you've got.'

'This is just a lecture from a miserable tart, I am going.'

When I got home, I gazed into that mirror again. I could see nothing, just my own refection.

'Oh Martin, come home I miss you!' I laid on my bed thinking off all the stories my bed could tell. Why was I thinking of going out to meet someone else, I would feel awkward in my mind. I don't even want Les round. I had a sleep, before Tommy came home.

It was not Tommy that woke me, it was hooting on a car horn outside my house, I jumped up looking out the window, and there was a dirty car on my drive with my Martin just getting out. I rushed to the door and fell in his arms.

'Hold on I'm stinking.'

'I don't care.' He looked lovely, all ruffled wild and a bit dirty. He did not stink, if he did I did not notice. We embraced when seated, me on his lap, on my sofa, Jonathan has given it back to me.

'It has only been a few days but I have missed you Jen, thank goodness we're home. How is Thomas?'

'He's fine, I'm fine, I am now. I missed you as well.' I was pleased he was back, I did miss him, could Jackie be right am I in love? We cuddled some more.

Straight in, that is what he does, so I did.

'I went to your office.'

'Office, what my site hut what did you make of that?'

'I met Linda.'

'Did you, she's a dream don't you think, I bet she was pleased to see you.'

'She knows all about me.'

'Of course she does, and Colin the Chippie and Jason they all know about my Jenny and Thomas, you're not a secret are you? Did you meet them all?'

'No only Linda, oh and Hazel the young girl just briefly.'

'Crikey Hazel she drives Linda nuts, did you see her short skirts on a building site goodness, the men like it, but Linda screams at her.' Why was I worried what he would say, if he knew I was spying on him? He didn't care a toss that I went there.

'What did you think of the place, mucky?'

'Mucky as you say but a builder's yard, I got the impression it was friendly.'

'Liked it there did you, we will have you on the team yet'

What an idiot I am, he is lovely, I more than really like him, I feel strange a bit light headed, I must ask Jackie about that.

'Look love I do stink, I feel as if I do so I am going home to unpack and shower, get yourselves ready and tonight we go out with Thomas for a meal, you are not choosing, I will.

See you at seven o'clock, no school tomorrow is there so we can keep my mate awake.' A brief kiss and he was gone. I was facing that mirror again telling it thanks for bringing Martin home.

We had a lovely evening, he took us to a very posh place, Thomas was on his best behaviour and did not bolt his food or talk with his mouth full not to show Martin up.

Martin looked lovely, he did wash up well. He has a dark natural tan from working outside you couldn't get that from a bottle. His thick hair, no receding hairline, no hint of grey yet but it would one day, he would not lose his hair it would just change colour, a lovely smile and teeth. Hark at me.

He told me I looked lovely when he picked us up in a now clean car. I had made an effort and was pleased with the result, I felt good.

Mo Lily

Chapter Sixteen

The unexpected happened Mr Simmonds my boss developed jaw trouble and at one time they thought it was cancer, his doctor had him in hospital toot quick, leaving me to hold the fort. I did, apprehensively, working longer hours. It was not cancer but while at it they removed all his teeth, some disease or other that was not going to heal, the teeth would drop out one by one, so they took them all out at once.

Can you imagine poor man, the pain and the eating problems, and no smile.

The first thing, whatever the problem a solicitor confronts you with is a cheerful smile. Until his mouth healed and dentures were fitted, he could not face meeting clients and would not come to the office.

I became good at his work, I could not sign official papers but I made sure I got them to him for a signature if needed.

Fortunately, we did mainly house exchanges, not much court business. That was certainly out for me and passed on to another solicitor. The houses I was able to make the arrangements needed, calling in to see Mr Simmonds after work with papers for him to sign and his advice.

Martin was most interested in what I was doing and thought me very clever. Thomas not as happy as he turned into a latchkey kid, letting himself indoors after school. More often than not, he went with Sam into Rosemarie's house.

It took a long while for Mr Simmonds mouth to heal before thinking about having dentures fitted. During this time, he decided to call it a day and take early retirement.

I received a very nice fat bonus from the man, we parted in tears. Now I am left without a job.

A long holiday for me, it is great, I have this huge amount of money, I don't save any I used it as salary to keep me while I am not working.

This morning Martin left his, upon looking at it, rather expensive watch on my dressing table. I decided to pop it into the "site hut" office. He was not there, Linda was tearing her hair out, she had a pencil behind each ear and one in her hand.

'Hello love, bad day actually it's that Hazel, guess what I've done?'

'Tell me?'

'I sacked her, don't know what Mr Anderson will think but I couldn't stand her here any longer. All that is to be typed and she is out there for an hour talking to that Simon and him with his hands on her bare thigh. I would have sacked him as well if I had the right.' Not taking a breath as the phone rang she snatched it up 'Anderson Team' she rather shouted into it.

I looked at the pile of papers she indicated, flipped through them, taking my coat off I sat in Hazel's seat and before she finished her conversation I was half way through an estimate.

'You don't have to do that Jenny.' She said a little in horror.

'I think it will help, where are the envelopes?' I asked as I rummaged through

Hazel's desk draws.

'In the box there.' Linda pointed to a shelf behind me. I carried on so did Linda as the phone rang again. We worked together, I loved it, and there was a purpose for me. She was grateful.

Martin fell in the door with amazement.

'What's going on here?'

'We sacked Hazel' I said. "We" hark at me. Linda nodded from the phone.

'He's here now,' handing the phone to Martin, she said 'Bob.'

'Hi Bob, trouble, no I have it in my office, hold on. Transfer that Lin,' and disappeared into his posh end.

We carried on it felt normal, it felt right I enjoyed it. My pile of typing getting near completion, this was a doddle compared to solicitor's work.

'All done.' I said to Linda as she put a cup of tea and a biscuit down for me.

'I'll just take this into Mr Anderson.' Off she went with Martin's cup. I drank mine with gratitude.

'He asked me if you were still here and he wants a couple of biscuits.' She said on return, grabbing another couple of biscuits.

'Did he? Gives us the biscuits I'll take them in.' As I went along to Martin's office, she called out to me.

'I will hold all his phone calls.'

As I opened Martin's office door he held his arms open wide for me.

'I said you'd be part of the team.' I sat on his lap again, we hugged and kissed as he snuggled his head into my breast and his hand slipped under my skirt to rest between my legs he said into my neck.

'Oh God I love you!'

I felt a flush rush up to my head, I felt hot, what had he said I could not handle this.

'Martin the window, the workmen can see us.'

'You're off about windows again? Those men work better with a hard on.'

'Martin!' I shouted at him as I jumped up pulling my skirt down.

'Is this how you treat all the team?'

'Only some of them, Simon's not keen.'

Looking out the window, I could not see anybody, hopefully, we were not seen.

'What's that over there?' I asked him

changing the subject again, taking interest in a large building beyond.

'Our workshops, we make all our own fittings in there, especially kitchens.'

'I see.' Thinking this is not just a little builder's yard, much more went on here than I first imagined.

'Typing there today I can see your work is very interesting. Those three bungalows you are building in Crowthorn Road sound beautiful.'

'And Black Down Walk we are building six there, just the same all our fittings again, our kitchens, window frames, doors and stairs.'

'Stairs?' I queried.

'Well no, not in the bungalows but if we need stairs we make them. We never buy anything readymade, the team has all the profits.' This proud man sat there going over things in his mind.

'I'd better go Martin, Linda is holding up your calls and she looks rushed enough as it is without having to deal with them.'

'Does she, no Linda can cope, nothing she can't handle.'

'Don't take advantage of the staff Martin.' I said wagging my finger at him 'especially the secretary.'

'Okay ducks point taken I will buy her a box of chocolates.'

'No, you have seen the size of her, no chocolates.'

'She likes chocolates.'

'I bet she does. I will get something for you to give her.'

'Thanks love.'

'Extra cash is always welcome, money is what she is here for remember.'

'Oh and there's me thinking it was me she was after.'

'Bye.' I left laughing at him.

'Bye Linda I have to pick my son up, see you tomorrow.' I called as I gathered my coat and bag.

'Oh thanks.' She breathed.

Next day I went to the site hut again, the tray had more typing for me. Linda was pleased I turned up. Martin was gob smacked we ignored him and got much work done. I left early but went again the following day and the one after that.

It was great fun, far more interesting than the work at the solicitors, I even took a couple of telephone calls while Linda had her lunch break, not at her desk as she always did. She went into town and did a bit of shopping she never has time for that, it always has to wait until the weekend. I told her not to rush back if I could not manage I would make notes and she could deal with it when she got back.

You have never seen anyone so pleased she told me she felt sure she was leaving things in capable hands and would not worry. What a big fuss she must feel so tied to this job being here alone.

'You are part of the Anderson Team.' Martin told me that night while we were discussing a new project.

'No just while I am having a rest.'

'Some rest, I am going to pay you.'

'No you are not, I shan't come if you do that, I don't want to be employed by you for God's sake.'

They were a happy crowd and although I

did not admit it to Martin, I did feel part of his team. Not all the Anderson Team are top tradesmen as Martin likes to think.

There was Percy! An older man almost old enough to be Martin's father, he had been a friend of his fathers. They worked together when Martin was a child.

An excellent carpenter, with much knowledge in most trades he graduated to site foreman or manager, whatever, always in charge. He liked a drink, a few unfortunate things happened in his life, his wife's death and Martin's father's death, leaving him to cope alone without these people around him he turned to the bottle for company.

When Martin first started the Anderson Team, he took on Percy and was pleased to have him in the team. Percy came with a friend, a labourer to fetch and carry for him, he treated him abominably, but they remained friends and could never work without each other.

Percy's drinking habits were catching up with him, not drunk in the mornings but certainly hung-over. Snappy miserable, unbearable to work with. Paddy his labourer friend took the worst of his bad temper they argued nonstop.

Percy called him some choice names.

After his liquid lunch at the nearest pub, he mellowed into a drunken incoherent idiot. This image was not good for the team. However Martin could not bear to dismiss Percy to him he was like an uncle, he had always been there, outliving Martin's mother and father, pickled with his booze consumption he would outlive them all.

Martin carefully chose the places he would give Percy to work. Always empty sites and often the drains or such. He could not be trusted with carpentry any longer. Other tradesmen did not like working with the them, so keep out of their way. With Martin's instructions, they were to keep an eye on Percy while you are there.

Because of this, different tales was reported back to Martin, about Percy and Paddy. Their work, their arguments and strange conduct including Percy and his drinking habits, but none was as funny as the hole.

Paddy had to dig a hole long and deep enough to accommodate a drain and a manhole. In the morning, Percy gave him instructions, measuring the area out for him where it was to be, he marked it clearly for Paddy where to dig, then left him to it.

He was a good labourer, strong and fit he soon was stuck into digging the hole.

'How deep do you want it Perc?' asked Paddy. Percy found a stick, which came up to about his hip.

'This deep.' Throwing the stick at Paddy, he went for his lunch.

Paddy did not take a break he kept digging. The two electricians who were sent there by Martin occasionally observed the hole digging. They sat on the roof to eat their lunch in the sun.

'He's digging that trench deep.'

'Yeah wonder why it has to be so deep?' They carried on eating. Soon they could not see Paddy, just his shovel and the dirt he was throwing out.

Percy tottered back from the pub, resting on the wall every now and then before he attempted a few more steps he was that bad. As he went to disappear into the hut, Paddy called out to him that the hole was finished and he was to "take a look".

When Percy see the depth he had made the hole, he nearly fell into it with astonishment, maybe it would have been better if he had. Paddy was called all the stupid idiots going, where's your stick.

In his confusion, Paddy had picked up the wrong stick and the one he chose was longer but a perfect fit to the depth of the hole now dug.

With some very bad abusive words, even to be heard on a builders site, Percy told him to fill it in and bang it down firmly to this size, giving him the original stick again. The electricians at one time thought Percy was going to hit Paddy with it.

'Why use a stick can't he give the man the measurements?'

'I don't think Paddy can read.' They continued to watch making a note to tell Martin.

Percy slammed into the hut, put the electric fire on and went to sleep.

When Martin enquired what was

happening at the site they relayed the incident. Martin raising his eyebrows sighed and thought no more of it.

However, that was not the end of it.

The next day Percy more sober, if ever he was anywhere near sober, incidentally still managed to drive his car to work, leaving very late when the roads were quiet, after a sleep he felt he could drive home.

He arrived in a foul mood and immediately released all his venom on to Paddy. Their arguing went on all morning, with much reference to the large hole. The base of the hole had to full with concrete. Again Percy leaving Paddy alone to do this. Percy was still being abusive to him as he left for his liquid lunch at the pub.

Paddy by now had his temper up, he mixed the cement in no time, barrow loads of it. The electricians taking their lunch in the sunshine on the roof again, watched.

When he had mixed all the cement that he needed, he went into the site hut and struggled out with a large toolbox, full with tools, which they found out later belonged to Percy.

He tipped the lot into the hole, he took the box and put a hammer to it and threw the box remains on their bonfire.

He wheeled his barrow loads of concrete over and poured the concrete on top of the tools, one load after another.

The electricians watching were in hysterics. Paddy smoothed the top over neatly to the right depth checking it with the right stick. Dusted his hands together with a great smile.

Percy returned, rolling along the churchyard wall for support again. As usual, he disappeared into the hut for the rest of the afternoon. Paddy sat in a deckchair he had found somewhere and was looking at the girlie pictures in the newspaper.

The electricians had trouble concentrating on their wiring, they were still laughing.

The next morning they heard Percy yelling across the site.

'Paddy have you seen my toolbox?'

'Ere, he's started' yelled the electrician to

his mate.

'No boss.' Said Paddy in a nonchalant manner not looking up from the bonfire he was poking, he was tidying the site.

There was a long pause as Percy searched further for his toolbox.

'I've looked everywhere, where's my bloody tools?' Scratching his head and looking around he went back into the hut.

'Strange that.' Paddy said. Percy came out again getting cross.

'You've had 'em, haven't yer? Took my toolbox home with yer.'

'What on me bike?'

'You've took them somewhere.'

'I tell you what Perc, your tools haven't left this site.' The electricians were bursting with laughter and still doing the same when they related this episode to Martin.

Martin had to laugh himself. He could see no answer to all this and thanked the men for reporting to him.

I was told the story so was Linda who knew them both better than me.

'I can't sack him and I can't employ him.' Martin told me sadly remembering the worker he was. For a few weeks, Martin sent a young man to the site to be their minder, not to work much, but just to keep an eye on the pair of them, see they came to no harm or did not do any damage.

This was proving to be costly.

Unfortunately or maybe, it was fortunate it stopped. The police caught Percy as he left the site one night, he was over the alcohol limit for driving and lost his license that meant he could not get into work anymore. Paddy joined him and also left. Percy stayed at home drinking his life away. Martin sent him money occasionally and Paddy paid him many visits.

Paddy has never touched alcohol, he has always been a teetotaler, his religion and his Irish upbringing from his mother forbade him. Watching Percy, he knew his mother had been right.

We all went to Percy's funeral, I had met him once or twice.

Paddy cried unashamedly all through the service, he placed on his coffin a small carpenter's plane, he said as they lowered it.

'Forgive me.'

Martin said it was like burying his dad all over again.

We had Mandy again that weekend she was quiet.

'Something up love?' I asked her.

'Nana's not well, she went to hospital in an ambulance.'

'That's fine, no need to worry, that is where we all go to get better.' I told her.

'Last night she was crying, I had to stay with Rene next door.'

'Well you are here now love, so let's put a smile on your face 'eh?'

'Okay.' She, thank goodness, cheerfully said. I told Martin he made a phone call to her house to see if all was well and to ask should he bring Mandy back as planned or keep her here for a few days. There was no answer.

'What did he say when you collected her?' I asked Martin. He did not see anyone Rene next door came out with Mandy, she said nothing about her grandmother.

The next day early, Martin had a phone call on the lines of:

'I say old chap could you keep the 'em

child there for a bit, my mother you know, not at all well.'

'I am sorry to hear that, I hope she is well soon, can you manage?'

'Yes, yes of course I can manage it is just 'er her, my mother is worried.'

'No problem I'll keep her all week bring her back next weekend, how's that?'

'Fine, thanks old man, I will say you offered the whole week, jolly good.' Martin told me word for word what the prick had said, even the 'ems when he couldn't bring himself to say Mandy's name.

'A whole week Jen how about that you go and tell her.'

'No you.'

'I will take a week off.'

'You can't do that she can stay here, she has to go to school now, I will take her it's not far.'

'Thanks Jen, I will pick her up.'

'I can do that as well, go and tell her and Thomas.' They were in the garden, I watched as Mandy hugged her dad, then she and Thomas did a little ring dance holding hands with happiness.

We made sleeping arrangements for her, when she came for the weekend Martin always took her home to his house to sleep.

She had the choice my little bedroom to herself or share with Thomas, they decided she was to be in with Thomas.

Back came the other part of the bunk bed, Mandy slept on the bottom as Martin made a contraption that would stop Thomas from falling out, though he assured me he was a big boy now, I had forgot, and he would not fall out.

Martin made another phone call asking for clothes and school uniform and shoes, anything she needed. He made a visit that evening and collected two bags from Rene next door.

The whole week felt like ages but went quick. Martin took her back on Sunday at five o'clock as usual we all had sad faces.

Martin came home in a rush from taking Mandy back to her grandmother, excitedly waving a piece of paper at me.

'Read it, read it!' He shoved the paper in my face as I took it I could see by his face it was something good. It started:

"Now mother is home I feel she will not be able to manage the child.

It is your turn to have her, do not make excuses she has done her bit.   O"

'Martin what does this mean?' I read it again taking in every unexpected word.

'It is my "turn" huh, she is not a game where you take turns in having a go. That is what he thinks. What sort of prick is he?'

'Martin stop, this means Mandy is ours they do not want her. What did he say?' They never spoke to each other much, just grunted as usual.

'Nothing he just gave me the note and said read this when you get home and let me know, that was all.' Not waiting until he got home dreading it was bad news and they were moving away, he stopped the car opened the envelope and read his note.

'Mandy will never go back she will stay here with us.' He snatched the scrappy piece of paper from me we read it again together.

'Why has he put O on the end?'

'O for Osmond, that's his name'

'Oh, I hate that name, I like Prick better.'

Martin smiled at me his arm round my waist still looking at the note.

'It does mean she can stay doesn't it? "My turn" he says look. Oh Jenny I can't believe it, she can stay, we will make a home for her.' We hugged each other, I cried with joy so did Martin, in fact he sobbed.

'Jenny will you marry me, will you help me make a family? I love you so much.'

Gasping I answered this dear sweet man.

'Yes thank you Martin. I have never been married before.'

'Neither have I.' We said no more just held each other. Jackie was right I am in love!

'She must stay here, still share the room with Thomas until she is settled she can have the small room when she likes but I have to make room for her clothes and toys.' I was planning and moving things around in my head, clear out some junk, plenty of that to move.

'Is Thomas asleep yet?' asked Martin

'No, not even in bed, doing homework I believe.'

'Let's tell him.' We ran upstairs.

'What have you two been up too now?' he asked as he could see we had something to say and we were both eager to tell him.

'Mandy is coming to live with us for good.' Thomas was astonished.

'She must sleep just here.' Pushing his stuff out of the way, he started to make room for her.

'We need a bit more room than that Thomas, this will do but it will be just for now, she must have her own bedroom, we will clear out the small bedroom of your stuff that you don't need anymore.'

'And paint it pink.' said Thomas.

'Pink?'

'Yes girls like pink.' Of course they do, this was going to be different for me. A little girl.

'Oh Martin.'

'Over a cup of tea in the kitchen all three of us sat feeling very happy making plans, Martin suddenly stood up.

'Jenny I can't stand this I have to go back for her, she must come here now.'

'I was just thinking how sad she must be there at this moment, and not knowing what we are planning for her.'

'I'm going to get her I will phone the prick and give him warning, I want all her clothes and toys, everything that is hers.' He was breathing fast and looking worried.

'Don't worry Martin if he wants Mandy to go he will be pleased to get rid of all her belongings, he will co-operate I am sure, but hurry before she is put to bed.'

He made the phone call to Mandy's uncle, he agreed, half an hour was all they needed, not believing their luck. Martin went, I continued preparing for her, making room for I had no idea how many clothes or toys.

We would manage, Thomas was already clearing out his cupboard making room. I did not realise he had so much that he did not really need.

She will always sleep in our house, Martin is here more often than at his own. Except at weekends when we go to Martin's beautiful home. I will take her to school, a bit of a trot, but not too far. No.

She must change schools, yes, that is it, I

will get her into Tommy's school no problem, she will like it there. Moreover, Thomas will certainly like her being there. They would go to school together, in different years, of course as Thomas was in the junior school and Mandy in with the babies, I wonder how long that will take to arrange.

Thomas was excited, I don't know how I felt, I was not worried, it was all happening so fast. I kept looking out the window for them, it seemed ages.

Then I lay down on the bed thinking, I had said I would marry Martin, I can't believe it, me, married. I did want to marry him, yes I did. Mrs Anderson, phew, what are we up to. Thomas came in my room and lay on the bed with me.

'Are you all right Mum?'

'Yes dear I am very happy.'

'Because of Mandy?'

'Yes but because of something else as well. Martin has asked me to marry him and I said yes I would.' My son sat up and looked at me wide eyed.

'How did you manage that Mum?'

I was just about to grab him when we heard the car toot. My daughter, Tommy's little sister had arrived. Our lives were never to be the same again, it was so easy and enjoyable to adjust to living with this little scrap of a child, a bundle of joy ready made for us all to share.

Martin wanted it official, so did the prick, the grandmother was too poorly to care one way or another. We assured her she would see her granddaughter as often as she liked. All arrangements were made, with a solicitors help, we adopted Mandy, I have a daughter and Thomas has a little sister who he guards with his life.

Thomas gave me away at our wedding and Mandy was my bridesmaid, it was a beautiful wedding, I think other people were there but I never noticed them.

Just Martin and my two children were with me. We now live in Martin's beautiful house, he said he did often think it was a waste of time building it. All along, he was hoping one day he would live there with his family and here we all are.

I still help Linda in the office, but my job is to look after my husband and children.

Mandy never talks about her grandmother. Neither she nor her uncle has ever asked to see her again. I did worry for a while that she was going to miss them and maybe would feel the need to make visits, but there was no fear of that. I cannot imagine how she felt, living there with them. Perhaps not unhappy, but just left out of things not fitting in at all with those older people, so alone, a father she adores but kept away from him too much, and never having a mother, poor kid.

Now she has me.

My daughter, Amanda calls me Mum just as Thomas does. Sometimes Mummy like little girls often do. I find I nearly always refer to her as Amanda. They have changed schools yet again to be nearer to this house. Thomas still manages to see Samantha, she comes to stay or he visits her.

However, it is a friendship that is waning, it started too young to last they will both gain experience with other people but I hope always remain friends.

We had a honeymoon in the South of France, which made me laugh. I told Martin about Peter, he thought it funny but was not really interested.

We still see a lot of Jackie and Bart, he considers Martin as his boss, and I suppose he is.

A completely different type of boss, he would never tell me to "Stay there" he would be the one to stay there and wait for me without question.

I love him so much, too much to put it into words here. Sorry!

Also available by Mo Lily

Turning
A road that leads you away from the road you are
travelling on
Alicia McKenzie-Fife is leaving her husband Michael after he
physically abused her in a public place then abandoned her when he
realised they were overheard.
The eavesdropper was none other than his Company Chairman

This is my Turn
Schoolteacher Sandra Ross, after nursing her failing mother
felt she could not return to teaching those ungrateful kids.
She would leave London, move to Cornwall, to live there alone.
However, after inheriting her murdered sister's obligation, she
would no longer be on her own.
She never contemplated sharing with anyone.

A Pint and a Push
The first story about these characters starting when they had
just retired, had no money, and could not afford a pint.
How they became wealthy, the funny and sad things that
happened to them.

A Port and a Push
the sequel
The same characters but their wives' story.

Just the Ticket

Jasmine has the six numbers and the ticket to prove it.
Her husband and nine children let the thought of so much money
turn them nasty, greedy and out of character.
Jasmine reconsiders claiming her millions.
She denied she ever had a ticket it was lost or never acquired.
She would wait until a more appropriate time to own up,
it turned into years.

Partners even when we Dance

Jean and Grace live together, they complement each other in a
comical and loving way.
Jean is a teacher of dance to all ages.
They were both married, had children, then leaving their
unsuitable husbands started a new life.
'I am not a lesbian for Christ's sake I have a child'
Jean has two boys, Grace a daughter who she never sees until her
unannounced arrival.
She came to visit her mother but did not leave.
This is their funny story.

The Day I Killed the Cat
Life through men's eyes.

Single Mums – Gawd Bless 'Em
Life through women's eyes.

Mo Lily

About the Author

Mo Lily lives in Dorset England with her husband and two elderly cats.

She was born in the East End of London and although she has lived in Dorset for many years, she still considers herself an East Ender.

As she is profoundly deaf, the written word is very important to her, television subtitles, telephone text and of course books.

Single Mums – Gawd Bless 'em

Made in the USA
Charleston, SC
31 October 2013